The Tattoo Hunter

The Tattoo Hunter
A Novel

Juvenal Acosta

Translated from the Spanish by
Janet Casaverde

GATO NEGRO BOOKS

Creative Arts Book Company
Berkeley • California

The Tattoo Hunter
is published by Gato Negro Books
and distributed by Creative Arts Book Company

Originally published in Spanish as *El Cazador de Tatuajes*
© Sansores & Aljure, Mexico City

For information contact:
Creative Arts Book Company
833 Bancroft Way
Berkeley, California 94710
1-800-848-7789

Library of Congress Cataloging-in-Publication Data

Acosta Hernández, Juvenal.
   [El Cazador de tatuajes. English]
   The tattoo hunter: a novel / Juvenal Acosta; translated from the
Spanish by Janet Casaverde.
      p. cm.
   ISBN 0-88739-496-5 (alk. paper)
   I. Title.
PQ7298.1.C76 C3913 2002
823'.64--dc21

                                                     2002023767

Printed in the United States of America

In Memoriam:

Juvenal Acosta Cruz, and
Aarón Hernández Montaño

What able bodied man...
does not wish...
to bedevil his ecstasy?

Donatien Alphonse François, Marquis de Sade

The Tattoo Hunter

A TATTOO IS NOT A SIGN IMPRINTED UPON THE SKIN, but rather upon the idea that one has about oneself. A sign made from desire, the tattoo is a scar. The readable product of desire.

This is the decade of the tattoo.

I have seen and touched, kissed, licked, bit, an infinite number of tattoos. Some of them in the most unsuspected places. In my archives of signs and scars I keep a tattoo shaped like an arabesque; the mark of a doubt; a phrase wilted by the passing years; a moon in the shape of a question mark; a musical line of Piazzola; the unanswered question of a labyrinth; a question mark in the shape of a moon; an eye that is a penis that is a vagina that is a cat; initials and numbers; angel wings on shoulder blades; Mercury's wings on ankles that are bridges to the Summer; golden branches on ankles that are bridges to the South.

I have kissed tattoos on breasts, on necks, on pubis', on backs, on thighs, around navels, on arms, on wrists, on foreheads; tattoos of shade and light in the very center of the eyes.

This is the decade of the tattoo because it is the tribal decade.

The resurgence of the tribe evidences the decay of the nations, the weary state of Western culture, the honest fatigue and the legitimate desire in each one of us for erotic and intellectual freedom.

The contemporary seducer is a tattoo hunter.

I DON'T KNOW HOW MUCH TIME HAS GONE BY. Aside from this awareness of my motionless body I feel nothing. The voices come and go, like the images I evoke so as not to die. To remember in order to survive. To die in order to stop remembering, to leave behind the footsteps, the gestures, and the signs. I do not want oblivion. In this bed, I project upon the veined screen of my closed eyes the memories, the longing, and the evasive silhouette of certain bodies. I don't have now, and never had, a god to appeal to in these times. I am not even sure whether I regret the lack of a deity.

I remember so that I may survive. I must give muscle firmness to a name. Four names among hundreds. I have four names that mirror four cardinal points and four elements—four simultaneous seasons of my life. Four velvety petals that together create a delicate orchid of carnal desire. Four names that sing of four faces. Each name is a question but not necessarily an answer. Each name is all the words and all the silences. Each name is Babel.

In each of these four names is the key of a secret that

is still off limits to me. That is the secret I intend to decipher before this fortunate lucidity abandons me. In the unveiling of the secret, in the process of undressing each circumstance that brought me here, I will try to answer questions I never articulated before, for I was too busy feeding my own egotistical appetite. This slow death cannot be other than the consequence of my endless desire.

IT BEGAN AS A GAME.

Later, words that never had any special meaning for me began to take on life. Words like panther and velvet. Words that brought about a feeling of pain and love mixed together. Words that tell of things we think just happen and then weave themselves around us; trap us in a spider's web of half-satisfied longings and an insatiable curiosity.

That is why now I am here, trapped in my body, this broken heir to that curiosity. Every now and then I listen to how they talk about me, as if I were just another object in this room, locked in its deprived aphasic condition. And yet, the paradoxical object that I am continues to think. With its minuscule leftover of a soul, it thinks that life is never ironic but fair. Fair because after using as objects of pleasure the many women who loved me, or who were with me without loving me, we—my body and I—have finally become the true object, the object par excellance. I, locked in my silence and in my conscience. It, truly besieged by its epidermis without possible escape.

It began as a game.

At the beginning it was an innocent game. It always is, at the beginning. The game of life with its rites of passage so I could become a man. Survival rites, those dictated by biology and hormones, and those dictated by tradition and culture. And then something happened. I remember it with dishonest precision. It happened almost twenty years ago. It was an idiotic *accident*, which should have not happened. As in all accidents, mine seemed to occur without a reason. "A motorcycle and invisible oil on the pavement." That is what I repeated over and over again until I convinced myself. It was a senseless, unavoidable mishap from which the minor result was a large scar that left my chest marked forever. A scar in the shape of a question mark. The major result, the consequence of which was to become grave, is the question which I will try to formulate now, before this momentary lucidity escapes me again.

It began as a game.

The game continues like this: upon an imaginary table I spread a map. With my eyes closed I signal a cardinal point (a bruise?) on its surface. It is a sexual map. That is to say: an invisible map of emotions and anxieties. A map made of soft skin and amber-colored liquids that run down from vanished thighs. A map of intelligent, generous, strong women. A carnal code of gestures and of signs.

But this is also a map of contradictions and deceit, of pain deep as a woman's body, deep as sleep or the suspicion of death.

IF I MUST RESCUE, one by one, all the women that came into my life, then I must choose, discriminate, run through the filter of pleasure names, eyes, smiles, hips, pubic hair, words. Run through the filter of memory our moments of joy, boredom, and sadness.

I don't know if I will get out of this. I infer from the comments of the nurses their sense of hopelessness. But if my prostration is a consequence of my excessive appetite, and if my appetite becomes the cause of my death, I must then bring those women back, restore their faces in my memory, their dignity, their prestige as women in the life of someone who only gave them words (such as these which I now think and which sooner or later death, the great mother fucker, will erase).

As a professor of literature familiar with two or three theories, I always assumed that seduction was not a part of the order which nature imposes on life, a cosmic, balanced, causal order. Seduction belongs to the order of artifice. It is an order that we invent and construct with codes and rituals, with signals, which we interpret according to our desires.

The order that governs nature is determined by the laws of survival. The order that regulates the precise and fragile mechanism of seduction is imposed on us by the laws of simulacrum.

What happens then when survival is based on simulacrum?

I decided—if such things can be decided—to be a man of my times. A citizen in the strict sense of the word: someone who belongs in a city. An urban being who finds security and peace of spirit in the sound of cars, buses, and the subway. In the purring of my computer hard drive, in the noxious exhaust of trucks, in the sight of plazas with cafes and casual people, the other citizens, my brothers and sisters. My sisters.

Seduction, intimate order of chaos, requires knowledge of the rules that organize the city and prevent its collapse. The strict order of the city must be respected so as not to alter its interior rhythm. There are laws—like the spontaneous law of entropy that makes possible for any type of relationship to function and then collapse—known, if not in a conscious way, in an intuitive way, by those of us who inhabit it. Through constant repetition, this organic movement becomes a kind of natural order, so ingrained in our blood that the environment of concrete and iron which we occupy finally becomes for us what woods are to a deer or a tiger. In the city, itself the greatest product of artifice, is where seduction, that other artifice, occurs in a more, shall we say, natural way. This is the first element of the trap: in the city only simulacrum, artifice, is natural.

THE MAP IS NOT THE CITY. It is not the territory, nor the men and women who occupy it, yet it represents them. In a similar manner, the contemporary city represents an idea of what we, postmodern beings possess of life.

A woman—always an unknown city filled with secret places, alleys, and windows—represents, like the map (symbol, model, abstraction) something that we would like to know, often with a certain sense of urgency.

(An unknown woman who walks down the street in the opposite direction and looks at you, and maybe smiles at you, is not asking for you to approach her, rather, she is making a quiet invitation to think about her eyes or her mouth as one thinks of a mythical city, far away, inaccessible. Every woman is an Ithaca of flesh. To love that woman spontaneously is to love the idea of the urgent, unexpected trip.)

The map, purest scent of geography, is also a guide to investigating the world to the core, an abstract possibility of escape, and a resource to orient oneself in case of confusion. But more than any potential "practical" purposes we may find for it, the map is nothing more than the simple representation of something infinitely complex, intangible almost. The search for meaning of that representation, of that set of signs, is what has ultimately imprisoned me in the silence of one condemned to death.

Woman: dangerous city that I did not survive.

I POINT MY FINGER AND IT FALLS UPON MARIANNE.

The memories I keep of Marianne include cups of Thai black tea, her short blond hair, and the open landscape of her body before me.

I met her on a misty Autumn night in New York City where the sound of a jazz band had stopped me—as only certain qualities in light or sound can stop people—in front of the entrance of a club where Benny Carter and his band happened to be playing. Something in my attitude as I simply stood out there under the light rain must have captured the attention of the English photographer. When I felt the lightning of the flash, I turned toward her and another flash blinded me. Upset by her boldness I demanded an explanation. She gave me much more than that. Half an hour later, espresso and cigarettes served as props as we began to know each other.

I was in New York for a few days to attend a conference and give a paper on eroticism in Latin American fiction. For the first time in my life I was enjoying a sabbatical and my only contact with academic life that year would be a couple of conferences I was to attend. Marianne lived in London, although she lived everywhere, as I would later find out. She was in Manhattan because the publishing house for which she worked had sent her to take pictures for a book on jazz to be published later that year. She had been taking pictures at the club all night and had stepped outside to smoke a cigarette when she saw me. I was listening to a version of the bolero "Rosita" that brought back some childhood memories and made me close my eyes. It was raining lightly and the water that dripped down my face, my attitude, captivated by the piano, made for a good photograph, she explained.

Marianne always dressed in black. She wore no bra because her young, small breasts did not need one. To my surprise she shaved her armpits. My experience with many of the Northern European women I had known was that they let the hair under their arms grow and, under the condition that they were clean, I found that very arousing. There is something exquisite and contradictory about a beautiful woman who does not shave her underarms. One is used to Latin American women shaving and when, suddenly, the nudity of a foreigner exposes one to that hidden tuft of hair, the association with the pubic hair is immediate. It is like finding another female sex hidden in each armpit. A gift for one's senses of touch, sight, and smell.

I also remember her with Tom Waits songs because we used to stay up until the wee hours of the morning, touching each other and listening to the first albums of the poet of Los Angeles. *Muriel, since you left town...* Marianne took me to her hotel that night and became very enthused about my Mexican stories and my recounting of childhood memories in the Tierra Caliente, the hot lands, of Guerrero (where I still used to go because my father was born there and that poor, arid region of Southern Mexico was my last contact with my earthly origin). While I told her stories about that violent Macondo, she heated water on the stove of the hotel kitchenette and gave me black tea to drink all night long.

Perfection, such as it manifests itself in memory, is always made of small imperfections. I remember that when Marianne slept her breathing emitted an irritating whistle that I now miss. When she was awake her sky blue eyes were a light in the middle of the dark, gothic cathedral of a New York City night. For me that light was an absolute truth because it antagonized the darkness of sex and of dreams. Nothing more real and crude than sexual darkness, nothing more uncertain than the simple anticipatory desire produced by the blurred image of a woman in semi-darkness. What sex has of direct and naked, desire has of elusive and veiled.

I found her on a Wednesday and we were together until Sunday. On Thursday morning I returned to my hotel and checked out. I joined her in her hotel room. I needed to be with her every hour of the day and night. I would leave her in the mornings to walk across Washington Square Park and get good coffee, stepping around dog and pigeon shit, avoiding being run over by early morning skateboarders, but all I wanted was to be back in bed with her. The day I read my paper at NYU she came. Although her Spanish was not very good, she demonstrated by her attention to my words that anything that came from me was important to her. Later, with my paper out of the way, I decided to ditch the conference so we could explore together the small wonders of the city. We marveled together at what was once the island of Mannahatta, named that way by the first and true Americans, and is now the capital city of the world. As we walked, she would suddenly wander away from me to take pictures of old doorways and stained walls. We liked to stop in abandoned alleys and walk hand in hand looking for a cafe hidden in that urban labyrinth which, like her London, is full of unsuspected sepia corners.

As the days went by we both felt a growing happiness at the feeling of having found each other by chance in an unexpected place. But isn't that how the most important things in life usually happen? Nobody who searches really finds. The search is a product of neurosis; the encounters, on the other hand, are the product of that universal law that leads us towards where we have to go. Nothing is casual. She, us, was the reason why I had to listen to the piano and stop under the light rain ("Misty," like the song) in front of the jazz club, and she had to go outside to smoke a cigarette. That order which takes us from one place to another, that order of chaos, of intuition, was what put us in front of each other.

We would have to separate once Sunday arrived and

we both knew that our long kiss of several days had to end. Saturday night she stared into my eyes and after taking a brief sip of her tea she suddenly said to me, "I want to have your babies." I felt as if I had been hit by something unknown and I immediately blushed. I extended a hand towards her womb as something inside of me so overwhelmed me that I felt like crying. Nobody had ever wanted to have children with me. I had never thought of having any and her declaration was one of such love that I knew then, in that instant, that some part of me was fractured forever. Both of us began to cry.

I had to return to San Francisco at dawn. I had my commitments and my cats, my apartment in Noe Valley, my bills, my friends, my clothes at the dry cleaner, my simulacrum of normality. I had too many paper and plastic etceteras, too many obligations that demanded my presence on the other North American coast. Her hands caressed my hair and I buried myself between her breasts like a child who buries himself in his mother. "Come to London with me," she said. But in reality she said something else. She said, "Be a part of my life, travel with me throughout the world, you will write the most beautiful travel chronicles and I will take pictures of Arab children, Balinese boats, Cuban prostitutes. Let's travel, let's go away together, you with your laptop computer and me with my cameras. Let's travel the world like gypsies."

IN THE MIDDLE OF THE FOG of my ill consciousness I hear someone who is talking about me. "They brought him in unconscious. A stroke. It was a very attractive woman. She had a tattoo and wore black velvet." My body feels so heavy. I don't know if my eyes are open. The voice must be that of a nurse. It must be one of those voices that I cannot distinguish from those of my ghosts. Stroke. Broken body. "She left him and then she split. Goner."

Black velvet in the emergency room of San Francisco General Hospital. All a sign of destruction, all a question mark. Waiting room of death and life. Coldest room. A woman wearing velvet and tattoos. I know who she is, but I don't know her name. I almost know her. Broken flesh, perfume of sweet Spanish moss now departed, touch of her fingers, smoky hair. Palace of flesh now in ruins. Smell, incense, candles. Fingernails sunk in skin. Fingers sunk in every hole of her submissive body. Consciousness in ruins.

WHAT IS THE BODY if not the problematic translator of our instincts, our needs, and our desires?

I, who always loved the human body and the perfection of the skin, the hardness of muscle, the flexibility of the limbs, had the misfortune of having to live with this scar for most of my adult life. That was the first fucking irony: living with a scar I found so repulsive that when I finally put myself back in circulation after the accident, it took me a long time to muster up the courage to take my clothes off in daylight or in the intimacy of a shared room. I would explain to the woman who was ready to undress in front of me that I had an unpleasant scar and almost with fear I would let her unbutton my shirt. I used to look for some sign of repulsion, something in her eyes, a contraction of the ocular muscles that would reveal rejection or repulsion. It never happened. The most honest was a Brazilian girl who when I took my shirt off in a hotel room in São Paulo, whistled and said something like "What the hell happened to you?" with a huge smile to which I responded in kind and with a brief explanation: a motorcycle accident.

I confirmed, thanks to my scar, that women, in general, do not have the same hang-ups as men do and look for something different in a physical relationship. Their connection with the male body is given in terms of something primal that transcends the body itself. The male surrenders (if he does so at all) to appearance, to the surface. The woman looks for something essential that is not defined by the perfection of the body: she surrenders to depth. The male is trapped in a classical Greek idea, which confuses interior with exterior beauty. He does not distinguish between them. According to this idea, if a woman is physically beautiful she has to be, by extension, good, intelligent, sincere, faithful, and other such stupidities that most of us men accept unquestioned. Women don't fall into that trap. They accept the scars because their gaze penetrates deeper than the skin, deeper that the wound on the surface of the body.

The second fucking irony is that of now being trapped in my body. I cannot talk, I cannot move, I do not have control over my physical functions. I shit and pee on myself and they have to change me several times a day.

But before its ruin my body was my entrance ticket to paradise. Thanks to it I was a sort of Narcissus who looked for an image in the waters of other bodies. But I was not someone content with the mere reflection of his own face; I was a different Narcissus, one who dissolved himself in feminine water, who allowed himself to be absorbed, seduced, by that clean, crystalline, transparent water.

I bent over those waters incited by my curiosity, more

than by any feeling of vanity. I bent over each one of those bodies as a victim of my own human nostalgia for paradise and for my melancholy. I bent over, thirsty for something more than water, in order to drink and be drunk in those mirrors of saliva and nocturnal moans. I didn't want to look at myself. I wanted accomplices of my search, witnesses of my anxiety. I wanted an echo.

That is why the irony is double. Now all the eyes that see me are witnesses to my ruin. Faces bend over the dry spring of my body and all they see is devastation. Nothing in me indicates that at some point in time the whole of my life was pleasure.

It is in ruin that I now understand that the abyss is truly on the surface.

NOBODY, EXCEPT SABINE and the woman with no name, knows that I am here. I have no idea how Sabine found out. I was so discrete that no one ever had any information about my love affairs or, in this case, my misfortunes. Sabine comes to visit me and she talks to me, but I cannot answer, even with a smile. She must sense that I understand what she tells me and stays for hours. Then she combs my hair and gives me a kiss on the forehead before leaving. I don't know when she arrived from Buenos Aires nor when she will leave. I don't know when she found out about all this. Her tears hurt me more than my own silence.

WHY MARIANNE?

Why is she the first woman to come to mind in this mapping of emotions and knots in the throat?

Maybe because she was my first sister.

Baudrillard gave me the key to this. Some years ago, in Mexico City while I was doing research for a long essay on the new Latin American novel, I got together with a Mexican writer, to talk informally about his latest novel, which dealt with the problem of seduction. That conversation left me with at least two matters pending, two issues that spun around in my head. The first had to do with the possibility of writing a female character from a masculine perspective, something that happened in this writer's book. The second had to do with matters of style: the fusion of prose and poetry in a middle point (much like the fusion of the masculine body—prosaic body—and the feminine one—poetic body—at an intermediate and absolute point during the act of love). Copulation and literature.

In search of answers I went to the library of the

University where I teach and found some old writings of Baudrillard in which he mentions by chance the "twin sister" of Narcissus. This truly surprised me. I had never heard of Narcissus having had a sister, much less that this sister was his identical twin. According to the story the Frenchman tells, Narcissus was in love with his twin. They both dressed exactly alike and even hunted together in the woods—what did they hunt for? When his sister dies (the cause of death is never explained by Baudrillard) Narcissus begins his agonizing daily ritual of contemplating himself in a pond. However, his purpose is not to find in the reflection of the waters his own image, as we have always supposed, but rather to look for the illusion of the face of his deceased beloved in the image of his own grief-stricken face.

The search of Narcissus is the search in himself for the other who has disappeared, has died, and is lost forever. The search is that of the impossible double, the impossible other. Narcissus' sister, dead and irretrievable turns into a deceptive image, barely sketched in the reflection of his face, and this delusion (what lover does not desire the bliss of delusion?), this game of painful mirrors becomes an irresistible vertigo which he himself provokes with certain unavoidable masochism, since it is in his own features that Narcissus finds the image of lost perfection, of love forever absent. Can there be worse torture than this?

Marianne was the first of my twin sisters. Of course that identification is strictly metaphorical. Marianne was blond, tall and had blue eyes. I am almost the opposite: dark, black hair, eyes darker than my hair. Like her, I always dressed in black, but maybe for different reasons. Perhaps to highlight the color of my dark skin or perhaps because, as a friend once told me: "Those who wear black are in mourning for themselves." My mourning was symbolic, but now that I may be dying the nurses dress me in white, as if they were preparing me for entry into paradise, a most unlikely probability.

Marianne showed me that we could be alike. It was not easy. To begin with, I am Mexican and this is, in principle, a terrible problem. I grew up with a ration of machismo I had not asked for. With a symbolic sombrero and a tricolor flag shoved up my ass as an unsolicited but mandatory sign of identity. When I left Mexico I became truly Mexican. When I lived there it had never occurred to me to think that I had to be Mexican, except on those days when we all are: Independence Day with tequila and shouts in the

Zócalo surrounded by drunken patriots. I became Mexican in a foreign land because the eyes of foreigners demanded me to be Mexican. Since then I have become the foreigner. I learned, in spite of myself, to be a full-time Mexican, and this meant tracing an interior dividing line—a border line of the heart—in order to look at my country from a distance and try to understand it; in order to question it with objectivity (with indifference?); and in order to hopefully some day attempt to establish which skin, which sentimental affiliation, which spiritual passport I would use to utter the words that travel from my heart to my mouth.

I learned—because I considered it indispensable to my apprenticeship as I became a foreigner and an adult—to reject that false identity which had been imposed upon me since my childhood. I learned rejection and I was left empty.

I stripped myself of that official version of my country like someone who avoids an unwelcome hug. I left that idea of Mexicanness behind me, as if it were a possessive, blackmailing, selfish mother. I wanted a change of skin and I was left empty.

Marianne gave me the key to a tribal identity I had sensed existed within me but didn't know how to articulate. With her I discovered a universal tribe made up of travelers, of expatriates and immigrants; of gestures and signs common to a few; of codes and attitudes she and I shared with other members of that tribe without borders. We had recognized each other because I was already starting to speak that clear, freer language. My nationless nudity did not make me vulnerable nor did it destroy me; on the contrary, it gave me the possibility of acquiring my own freely chosen identity.

Marianne came along and, without intending to do so, she welcomed me into the tribe that travels the world without hymns and without official ceremonies. She treated me as an equal member of that tribe and I loved her more for it.

TWO MONTHS AFTER MEETING HER in New York City, two months after watching her plane take off for London, Marianne arrived in San Francisco. She came to stay "for an indefinite amount of time." Her plans were, more or less, to obtain information about a Masters in photography at San Francisco State University; to work with a group of local photographers she had met in Prague; to take a short trip to the beaches of Southern California, and to take pictures of the human landscape of the West Coast. I suspected that these plans were also part of a strategy to be close to me, but I didn't ask any questions.

I picked her up at the airport and took her to my house where she stayed for a few days before leaving in my car to go to Los Angeles. There were two big photography shows she wanted to see: one by Tina Modotti and the other of Manuel Álvarez Bravo.

Her arrival was something that I had been anticipating with anxiety. Two months of e-mails, of phone calls at absurd times, of remembering our bodies entwined in her bed at the Washington Square hotel. Weeks and weeks trying to bring back her smell, above everything her smell. She smelled of Oriental fruits, of incense. Her body had the smell of a temple and in that temple my desire was the priest.

When she got off the plane and I saw her again I realized once again why I felt all that anxiety. At twenty four her beauty was remarkable. Her presence was emphasized by the absolute security she felt about the body she covered in black velvet. You could feel the effect of the black silk lingerie under the velvet. Her way of moving among that American mass of mediocre, tasteless appearance (compliments of The Gap and Macy's) could only be called sleek, because of the unintentional feline-like quality she possessed. Her hips were wide and her hair barely fell upon her shoulders like an aura around the face of a virgin in some medieval painting.

In my apartment my cats fell immediately in love with her and I loved her more for being finally there. She wandered through my space with curiosity. She stopped to look at my books, my compact discs, and my paintings by Vicente Rojo and Gustavo Rivera. Like a cat herself, she opened my closets, touched my coats, and smelled my shirts; her sense of smell began to appropriate that small geography, which she approved with a smile of confirmation. Then she asked for tea, which I thought I ruined because I did not know the exact temperature at which it had to be prepared; then she hugged me and told me that she did not want to interfere with my work and would leave when I asked her to do so. I loved her more for that.

When she went to the bathroom to take a shower, I sat in the living room looking at her luggage and the leather bag she used to carry her photographic equipment. I lit a cigarette and felt scared. I was used to living alone and suddenly I had in front of me the evidence that my freedom was being threatened. Her luggage, sitting quietly on the hardwood floor, was a mute declaration of love, but it was also the tangible proof of that which had been possible thanks to necessary chance, thanks to the universal law of encounters. Her luggage was the evidence that what we had was about to turn into something more defined, something controlled by the desire for the constant presence of the other and the human obsession for chasing away solitude. The mirage of the other was about to be destroyed. A falling stone was breaking the surface of the pond.

But when she came out of the bathroom, wrapped in my bathrobe and drying her hair with my towel, her blue gaze and her careful way of walking made me forget my worries for a moment. I hugged her and lead her to my bedroom where the bathrobe fell at the foot of the bed and I fell at the feet of my desire.

We went out for dinner every night. Sometimes, we would walk back home, stopping at Cafe Babar on the corner of Twenty second and Guerrero, where she would put coins in the jukebox to play songs by Patsy Cline, Tom Waits, and Tony Bennett. Marianne would drink a couple of Guinness's and I would ask for glasses of Chilean Merlot while we talked about movies, books, her trips. Those were days of wine and roses. We would return home and continued drinking until the wee hours of the morning. I had an endless supply of red wine and beer in my apartment. We would drink and listen to music, we would laugh and dance for hours, then we would fuck as if there were no future, as if the future did not exist. But we also fucked as if we knew that it would not last forever. We would continue drinking until dawn and tired of kisses and licking every inch of each other's bodies we would fall asleep without even touching.

WHEN MARIANNE LEFT FOR LOS ANGELES to see the photography shows two things happened that changed everything. The first was a feeling of distress because I realized that this new and brief absence had brought upon me a completely unexpected, but logical, feeling of relief. For those two months after we met I had wished to see her again with such intensity that now that she had gone for a few days I began to feel guilty for not missing her. Her arrival at my house had disturbed my daily rituals. The book of essays on the novels and short stories of Juan García Ponce which I had been writing for about a year—and according to me one I would finish during that sabbatical which brought more than unexpected events—had been tossed aside since she had entered my life with her impertinent flashes. At first, since she was in London, I had not been able to concentrate; I wrote her endless e-mails and listened for hours to the songs that reminded me of her as I drunk bottomless glasses of Kentucky bourbon. Now that she was in San Francisco and that all my time was for her I had lost the sweet habit of missing her. I actually began to miss the feeling of missing her. Her departure restored my routine and sobriety for a few days. I was thankful that my apartment belonged again to me and my cats only.

I did not miss her.

The second event was the unsuspected appearance of Sabine.

IN HIS *DIARY OF A SEDUCER*, Sören Kierkegaard, the Danish philosopher (and frustrated poet, although, how many philosophers are not frustrated poets?), tells us the story of a spiritual seducer, Johannes.

Johannes, Kierkegaard's alter ego, is a seducer who is more interested in the possession of the soul than that of the body. His sweet contender, Cordelia, is a delicate and inexperienced maiden (and aren't the true victims of all seducers just so?) who, like Johannes, is also the alter ego of a real person, Regina Olsen. Kierkegaard, in his youth, maintained a long lasting engagement with Regina, whom he met when she was only fourteen years old. Their relationship was never consummated, despite the desires of the impetuous youth, because as Kierkegaard himself has insinuated in the most discreet way in his personal diaries, he believed himself to be impotent. The fear of failure in love—and its implied intellectual failure—as consequence of failure in copulation made him cold and evasive, and this is precisely the way in which the protagonist of his book conducts himself throughout the narration of the Diary.

Johannes, unlike other archetypal seducers, is not a man of action, but rather a reflexive, intellectual seducer. What fascinates him the most about the ceremonial and delicate process of seduction is not the final result, logical and predictable, that is the deflowering, the passionate surrender, the defeated virtue, but rather the method itself; the gradual intellectual conquest of his adversary. What truly excites Kierkegaard's seducer is the *how* of the conquest, the process itself, not the outcome. Johannes is an authentic aesthete, an exquisite poet of seduction.

The work of seduction, the meticulous construction of that delicate mechanism, is only justified by the spiritual qualities and the virtue of his maiden, which he demands to be of the highest nature. Quality versus quantity. Only innocence is worthy of attention. The epigraph from Mozart's *Don Giovanni* that the Dane chooses for his book is more than significant, it is indispensable: *Sua passion predominante e la giovin principiante.*

In the notes that Johannes writes in his diary while he is occupied with the seduction of Cordelia, one immediately realizes how far removed this seducer is from that utilitarian vulgarity more characteristic of the vampire Don Juan:

> *There is no doubt that I am in love, but not in the ordinary sense, which is something that must be treated with great precaution since it may have dangerous consequences; in any event, this happens only once in a lifetime. Even so, the god of love is blind; one can trick him if one is a little astute. The important thing is to be as sensible to impressions as possible; to know what kind of impression*

one produces, and what type of impression one receives from each maiden. In that way one can fall in love with many women at the same time, in a different way with each one. It is not enough to love only one, and loving them all the same is undignified; but to know one's own capacities, and love as many as possible; to let the soul grow in full magnitude for love, giving each one of them the adequate food while they all shelter under the protection of a great conscience... that is a blessing for which it is worth living!

Johannes needs to exert absolute control of every single aspect relevant to the seduction. In this he is not different from the vulgar seducer. His purpose, in the end, is the same, to conquer and defeat. However, his method of seduction must be appreciated for its sophistication. Kierkegaard is a philosopher with the soul of a romantic poet. Thus, Johannes is a seducer with romantic roots, he is a pure seducer.

THERE ARE SOME WHO SAY THAT REALITY IS LIKE A BOOK, a multiple text—textile of meaning—but if we are ready to believe this we should then ask ourselves if there is a reality more difficult to read than that which weaves the indecipherable text of our sexuality.

In the case of the impure seducer, the *Casanova vulgaris*, the problem of how to read the woman-text is easily solved: the woman is read as a text of immediate consumption—a cheap romance story? A little porn magazine? In this paradigm a woman is always disposable and replaceable.

The problem with the first kind of seducer, the pure one, is complicated because his game can easily transform itself into an ethical problem. His seduction is always a conscious act, and it's never the product of sole instinct, but rather of intellect. His reading of the feminine text is not detached, it is always personal. This intimacy seduces him and thus involves him in such a way that it removes him from the frivolity of a common Casanova. The pure seducer goes after what a woman keeps in the depths of her soul; the impure seducer remains dazzled on the shiny surface of her skin. For the pure seducer the woman to be seduced is the fleshy result of his imagination in more than one way; she is the erotic investment of his deepest desires, of his most unspeakable fears, of his weaknesses. She is the fleshy result of his own discourse, and thus the wager has more of a risk since he has created a fiction with the broken pieces of his memories and his longings turning her into the incarnation of his neurosis and his traumas. The pure seducer turns into a kind of Doctor Frankenstein of seduction. Beware.

I AM NEITHER A CHIEFTAIN NOR A WARLORD. I am not a powerful man. But I am prostrate in what might be my death bed, claiming with my memory my lost empire.

Like Artemio Cruz, I hear voices around me. Unlike him, the voices that I hear talk about me in English, or talk in the language of indifference about other things, more important than my body that lays on this bed. Sometimes it's the voice of Sabine that fills the room with questions, but usually they are the voices of the nurses that clean my body or walk by doing whatever nurses do, or the deeper voices of the doctors who, like their counterparts all over the world, always manage to sound arrogant. Voices come from the hallway and are like echoes, sometimes I cannot tell them apart from those that arise in my dreams. Like Artemio Cruz, my body defeats me by my life, by my excesses, by my insatiable appetite, by my desire.

I think about Artemio Cruz and I automatically think about a symbolic, difficult grandfather. The Mexican from the middle of the century versus the Mexican at the end of the century. Another way of doing the same things. Or these things, are they really the same? I think about Artemio Cruz and I think about a country that is far away and dead for me.

When I left Mexico, thanks to the scholarship that Aunt Teresa had the good taste to give me before dying, I thought that I was not going to last for more than a year away from Mexico City. Dulce, my little girlfriend back then, threatened me with everything so that I would return as soon as possible. My mother undertook the task of sharing the gossip with me: as soon as I set foot on California soil, Dulce had become pregnant by the guy who is now her husband. I began staying in Gringolandia little by little. First my Masters, then the Ph.D., the struggle of finding a position at a good University, the easy life of California, and the comforts of the first world. At the end of all these years I found my ass installed in a cushy, well-paying job, with two or three students willing to go out with me after each semester was over, clothing from Nordstrom and Union Street, and money to travel more or less where I felt like it.

My relationship with Mexico changed. Two or three trips a year to visit my family, get together with writers to talk about their work, buy books. I watched, as time went by, how the corrupt people in power were fucking over the entire country. In everyday life, my relationship to Mexico became very much that of a spectator. I read newspapers and magazines on the Internet, and watched the news on mediocre Hispanic television. I ended up with a relationship with Mexico that was comfortable and filtered by distance and nostalgia, and a vision of my homeland as a painful, *fin de siècle* metaphor for the decline of the times.

However, I think the reason I ended up settling down in California had more to do with that unending flux of women who occupied my time and my head as the years went by. There was always someone to call, with whom to go out, from whom to run away at two in the morning escaping to my apartment and my bed where my cats awaited me.

I have clear memories of my messed up teenage years in Mexico. My parents had no money, but Aunt Teresa did. She had inherited lots of money from my grandfather (a Spanish immigrant who died swearing at Franco and the Yankees) and she adored me. I played the piano for her and wrote poems that rhymed; she saw me as a talented young man whom she had to support so that one day I might become "famous like Amado Nervo"—an obscure poet from the end of the 19th century. Her affection and her money made it possible for me to go to a private school in Mexico where, after a few weeks, it became evident that I came from a family without much means. I finished elementary school without major incidents, but high school and college were particularly difficult since I never had decent clothes or a car or money to ask a girl out to the movies or to have a drink. I rebelled and that rebellion consisted of isolating myself more and more. The parties, the excursions, the outings with the boys and girls of my age were chimeras. I had never gone steady with a girl until I met the ephemeral Dulce. I sought refuge in books and study. Then I sought refuge in alcohol and later in the older women I began meeting. For some years I turned into a wild bohemian. I ended up scorning those middle and upper class girls of Mexican society who were only interested in catching the whitest boy, the best dressed, from the best family, the one who drove the newest car, the one who paid for everything. I scorned them for being stupid and being whores, for being Catholic and hypocrites; because they preferred to take it up the ass before losing their virginity. I scorned them because none of them saw beyond my empty pockets and my discolored clothes.

SABINE. SABINE.

Nobody wished to get to know me as much as you did. Nobody wished to explore my abysses and failures as much as you did. Perhaps you wanted to be my sister because your origin was also a question. Since I met you, you came to my thoughts each morning and even in this time of disgrace I wake now and then from this nightmare thinking only about you. I met you in the best way possible, do you remember?

You were in that bar in San Francisco with two other girls your age. I was on my way to a party and had dropped in for a drink. I heard Spanish. No, I heard a Mexico City accent and walked over to your table. Are you Mexican? Yes, your friends replied, pleasantly surprised to find a countryman. You nailed your eyes into me and I still feel the pain. No, you said, I am Argentinean. I was invited to join the group and after a while I invited you all to a party at the house of some Brazilian friends of mine. You all declined and I had to say good bye. By then I had already decided that I had to see you alone, that I needed to know you. As if attending an order, a week later (would I find the Argentinean?), at the same time, you were at the bar, completely alone, reading, of all books, *Hopscotch* by Julio Cortázar. "How late in life you get to Cortázar," I came up from behind, kidding, and I repeated in one go and in its entirety, because I know it by heart, the one-page chapter seven of the novel. "I touch your mouth, with the tip of my finger I touch the outline of your mouth." You reproached me for teasing you about not reading that book before, and you were right: at twenty-three you had already read it twice. We each had a Cosmopolitan and went out into the night of the Mission District to talk about Argentinean writers, tangos (which you did not like because you thought of them as something old-fashioned and sad), and Charly García, all of whose songs you knew. Sabine, Sabine. You were Argentinean with French blood and a French name and your long hair falling about your back was a provocation, a declaration of war, a challenge to my good sense. You rejected my advances over the next thirty days, but you finally gave in to my words, to the slickness of a wolf that was older and more experienced than you.

There was no one in my life more beautiful than you, Sabine. No one had that smile, a waterfall of light, May dew falling from the tree of night, lightning of fingerprints on your olive skin. Under your young shadow I let my adult voice grow with the idea that some day, far away, I would have to settle down forever. I also abandoned, though much later and as a horrible sin, my Mexican prejudices against Argentineans, not only because I loved you but because in escaping from myself and loving you I suddenly saw myself arriving in the Buenos Aires airport, the Ezeiza, running away from myself and following the perfume of your skin, looking for the crystal of your laugh.

ONE CLOUDY AND TOTALLY ORDINARY AFTERNOON in San Francisco Marianne came back from Los Angeles tanned and happy. The shows had been worth the trip and she had taken advantage of her short stay and my car to escape to Santa Monica and Huntington Beach, where the nights are warm and the people a little like plastic. She came back and that sentimental and erotic order, established by her arrival from London, had already been altered by the unexpected appearance of Sabine. In spite of this, I was happy to have her once again by my side, to listen to her sexy British accent and her detailed descriptions of some of my favorite photographs by Modotti and Álvarez Bravo. I was also amused by her reaction to the beaches of Southern California, land of fake breasts, dyed blondes, and cheap beer. She told me about her quarrel with the police, caused by her habit of sunbathing without a bikini top. This is a country of peasants, she would often tell me. I liked the way she let herself be impressed by the frozen images of the photographers. I liked her opinion of a region of the state where I had lived for many years and now avoided with almost puritanical fervor. I liked having her among my things once again. I watched as she buttered a piece of toast, her back to me while, with my eyes, I traced her hips, her narrow waist, her naked shoulders. I liked the recent red and black tattoo in the shape of a panther on the back of her right shoulder. She did not have that tattoo when I met her in New York. She had gotten it done in Madrid and sent me a postcard which explained why she had inscribed her skin in my honor: "The panther, like you, is the only animal that emits an invisible fragrance which it uses to trap its prey." She was in love and so was I. But I had begun to feel divided.

I HAD NEVER LIED TO A WOMAN. Whoever thinks that lying is an acceptable strategy in a relationship between a man and a woman knows absolutely nothing about the feminine soul. I told Sabine about the existence of Marianne the very first time we went out together. I didn't hide anything, not my love for her, nor my fear of losing my freedom. But when Marianne came back from Southern California I didn't know how to inform her about my recent friendship with the girl from Argentina. It was explainable, but I was not able to phrase an explanation that did not hurt her. In those days I was supposed to have been working on my book about García Ponce; in her absence I was supposed to miss her and wish for her prompt return and nothing more. But, as my father used to say: "If you want God to laugh, tell Him about your plans."

I decided to talk to Sabine and explain the situation to her. Sabine, who by then was already getting used to my presence and insistent calling, told me that she would wait a reasonable amount of time until I figured out what I was going to do. I concentrated on Marianne as much as I could but one day I found myself pissed off because I wanted to speak in Spanish about a particular story by García Ponce ("El Gato") and I couldn't do so with Marianne. I began to resent her presence. I became an asshole.

Marianne confronted me: "What the fuck is going on? I thought you wanted to be with me, what the hell is wrong with you?" I didn't know what to say. I evaded the confrontation and shut myself in my study to smoke and have some red wine while I listened to tangos sung by the Uruguayan Julio Sosa, because tango is to the soul of a troubled man what French perfume is to the neck of a beautiful woman.

THE CAT GREW INSIDE OF ME.

On a random day some years ago I woke up, made myself some coffee, glanced through some pages of the newspaper and got in the shower. When I stepped out of it I looked into the mirror and saw my naked body, my scar in the shape of a question mark, my pubic hair, my semi-erect penis, my long hair, my broad shoulders, my dark skin, and my black eyes. I saw the panther years later Marianne would see.

The cat grew inside of me without me realizing it. My black clothes, my way of walking, my silences, my way of being elusive, arrogant, vain, selfish. All feline attributes, all tools of a dark trade, symptoms, all of them, of some contemporary, infectious, postmodern maladie.

My cats, two females and a male, always slept on my bed. Cordelia, Fuensanta and Legión. The first, like the Cordelia of Kierkegaard's seducer, is a cat of gentle and delicate nature; a kind of untouched, quiet, loving damsel. Fuensanta is electric, sensuous, sensitive to my touch and to sounds that I am never able to identify. The first time that Fuensanta came into heat (first and only, since I could not stand that experience and took her immediately to the vet to be spayed) she howled like a whore out of hell, like an irredeemable sinner. She would stick to my legs and rolled around on the ground while Cordelia avoided her and ran to hide among my books. Like the nameless woman who would destroy me, Fuensanta is an erotic, disturbing, and elegant animal. Legión is all the demons reunited in his elastic and wide body. He has a grim and malicious appearance, but of the three Legión is the most faithful, the one who understood my moods best when I was at home, and surely the one who misses me the most during this unexplainable absence. My cats are black like an accusation.

THE FELINE I WAS, without meaning to be, walked into the forest of the night, like the tiger of William Blake, but that forest was a sexual labyrinth whose walls are stained mirrors, sepia-colored fingernails, and certain guttural sounds.

How to draw the itinerary of a labyrinth? How to articulate what has no name?

> *And what shoulder, & what art*
> *Could twist the sinews of thy heart?*

Blake spoke of a multiple Tyger that blazes with intensity in the nocturnal woods. Huge tiger, undefined, whose unbearable stare is very much like the fatal embrace of the angel of Rainer Maria Rilke. Rilke's angel is feminine, but Blake's tiger is masculine. I imagine that these two could copulate and give us another creature. A beast for a more contemporary and darker mythology: an end of the millennium gargoyle, irremediably gothic.

But the cat is discrete and elusive. The cat is the tiger's sigh.

The tiger is so magnificent and powerful that a tiny cat

sprouts up from its every exhalation, like a god who makes his creatures in his image and likeness. Since it arises from the interior of the tiger, the cat is imbued of its electricity and its energy, of its grace and its instinct, of its intuition and its sensuality, of its elegance and its ocular barrier with the world. The cat distances us with its glance.

The glance of the cat is, of all the known signs, the most equivocal and indecipherable.

MARIANNE SENSED THAT I NEEDED TO RECOVER MY SPACE and decided to rent a room in the Castro, the gay district of San Francisco. I thanked her and dedicated myself to working and to missing her. I didn't look for Sabine immediately. I tried, uselessly, to concentrate once again on my work, on my book, on my life such as it had been before Marianne. As my attempts failed, I decided one day to go to Mexico. I didn't ask Marianne to come along; I told her I'd be too busy working on my research even though I knew that wasn't truth. I'm not sure why I left. Sabine was about to return to Argentina. Going to Mexico City at that point meant not being with her for two of the four weeks that were left before her departure. And still I went, thinking perhaps that a bit of Colonia Condesa, new Mexican cuisine, and aggressive smog would help me put a little order into my ideas. Also, I went because to flee is the privilege of the selfish.

Once installed comfortably in a small hotel in Mexico I dedicated myself to enjoy my favorite activities: getting drunk with my friends, looting the stands of the Parnaso and the Ghandi bookstores, getting together with writers in the restaurants of that infernal and delicious triangle of the Colonia Condesa where food has nothing to envy that of San Francisco, going to the new downtown clubs to dance, etcetera. I was to have two weeks of dissipation that, in my mind, would make me forget my American life, my obligations and, above all, the women I loved and didn't want to hurt. But once again the music of the days put in front of me a melodious voice, a look and a smile that stopped on me for two seconds longer than was appropriate.

WHEN I WAS A TEENAGER and no girl would give me the time of day I used to dream about meeting someone who didn't feel the right to humiliate me in return for her time and her kisses. The ritual of courting a young Mexican girl in my teenage years during the seventies and eighties was stupid and humiliating. I don't know what may go on these days among young people, since everything changes, but, at the time, my absolute lack of success among the women my age made me wish I knew a different type of woman. I had the vague idea, the intuition, that there were women in some part of the world who would listen, who would pay attention to my words, who would not see me as a creep who spoke of things which were unusual or different. I wanted to believe that someone awaited me in an unknown place and that in her own solitude she already awaited my arrival, she prepared for our future encounter. I was right. My intuition was always my most valuable possession, and life was generous by proving to me that the wait in that dull, middle-class environment had been worth it. Since San Francisco is a kind of condensed version of the world, it gave me the opportunity to get to know some of the most fascinating women of the world.

A friend asked me some years ago why never, during my adult life, had I had a love relationship with a Mexican woman. I didn't know what to answer in that moment but I think I remember feeling embarrassed and guilty. Days later I realized that to begin with no Mexican woman had wanted to have a relationship with me. That discovery hurt me because of its truthfulness. If no Mexican woman had dignified herself to love me, why the hell did I have to feel guilty? On the other hand, the possibility of finding a Mexican woman in California was even smaller than in Mexico City. And when I went to Mexico, even though I did so with certain frequency, I didn't have the time needed to meet someone. My stays rarely lasted more than two or three weeks at a time, thus, the normal duration of a courtship ritual, of simultaneous seduction, was never long enough for that click to happen.

To count women is an insult, not only for them but for oneself as well. This is why I would never dare to quantify my relationships. All of them have emerged from an enormous desire to know the other person, to know what she thinks, what music she listens to, what her lips taste like, what kind of books she reads. One falls in love out of curiosity. I don't remember a single case in which I did not fall in love, even a little bit, with a woman I seduced (or was their strategy of seduction to play at being the seduced ones?). I have offered my tribute of pain and pleasure to all my lovers. There were some who didn't love me; there were those who loved me as a friend and nothing more; there were some who lay by my side to sleep as sisters. There were the ones who loved me and ended up hating me. But there was always, at least on my part, passion and surrender.

That is why, when after fifteen years of not having fallen in love with a Mexican woman, I suddenly had before me the unequivocal signs of the look of Constancia entering my bones through my eyes, I felt something that was at the same time a feeling of emotion and disconcert which was, in truth, unknown to me.

THIS IS A SIGN that can be easily translated into poetry. On the other side of the table, in front of me, is Constancia, a painter from Monterrey, Enrique, a writer and friend of the family, and Margarita, Alberto's wife. To my left, Alberto, to my right a Frenchman whose name I can't recall. We speak in French out of courtesy to the nameless Frenchman, but the individual conversations are in Spanish. Constancia drinks her tequila with sangrita, like I do, and takes advantage of each sip to look at me. One always enjoys a splendid meal at Alberto and Margarita's house. The house is a tribute to the architect Luis Barragán and on the walls there are paintings by artists I recognize, like the ones by the Brazilian Bia Wouk, Francisco Toledo, others from Oaxaca. Nouvelle Mexican Cuisine. We finish eating and a maid comes into the dining room to announce that the coffee is ready. The coffee is served in the living room and I take advantage of this to sit by Constancia at the same time that I whisper into her ear, without anyone showing a bit of surprise, that I have something to tell her. She agrees with a nod and we speak with our hosts and the other guests for over an hour until Enrique, the writer, announces that he must leave to pick up his children; the rest of us see this as a cue indicating that it is time to go. Constancia is going towards the south of the city and I ask her for a ride to Coyoacán. I am not going to Coyoacán, I should actually be going in the opposite direction, but if in that moment she were to be leaving for Monterrey City, under some pretext I would go with her up to the peak of its highest mountain.

Once in the car I apologize for using the seat belt (ultimate sign of having become a gringo in the eyes of Mexicans) and we renew the conversation talking about nothing in particular. "How do you know Alberto and Margarita?" "Margarita is absolutely delightful", et cetera. We arrive at Coyoacán and I ask Constancia if she would like to have a cup of coffee with me. She says yes, and as we walk from the car to the plaza she asks me what it was I had to tell her. "That all things are timely. That I have three cats, and I am in love with two women who are in San Francisco. That I am writing a book about Juan García Ponce because I love his writing. That I always dress in black and I have an imperious need to get to know you, to smell your armpits, to buy you a book, to see the studio where you paint." Constancia stops and looks at me fixedly in the eyes: "If you are not talking seriously I think I should leave." She smiles, a little insecure. I take her right hand. I kiss it. I tell her that if she leaves, some day she will regret it. The night comes down slowly over the windows and the cobble-stoned surface of Francisco Sosa, my favorite street in Coyoacán. I kiss her hand again and when I raise my eyes I see that hers are closed.

This is a sign that I am able to translate.

MY CONSCIENCE IS TATTOOED. My tattoos are not on my skin (not true: I have kisses and scratches tattooed on my back). I have tangos tattooed upon the nostalgia of a mouth; poems tattooed on my apocalyptic anxiety; my chest was tattooed forever by a woman of water who inscribed upon it her name with menstrual blood and said to me, "You are mine motherfucker, only mine." A tattoo always tells a story. Sometimes the story is not of a tattoo but of a scar. But the scar is a tattoo. Scar: lightning upon the skin. Let me be me, let me be yours. The tattoo is a freely chosen scar.

Our love stories leave scars upon the skin of the kiss, upon the alcohol we drink, upon the uncertainty of the days that go by. Each morning our nakedness shows us those scars. But the tattoo is a marking of sovereignty upon the skin. An exclusive territory of shadows, a shadow of light, a bullfighting ring of epidermic calligraphy and melancholy. Calligraphy of sadness, of rituals fulfilled in the name of that modern pain created by the anxiety for freedom.

I have tattooed on my retina a painting by Magritte, a regret on my esophagus, a tongue on my crotch, a silence on the decade of the seventies. I have tattooed on my throat the words I did not say, the ones I spit, the ones that live in the uncertain future of my unborn children. Tattoos of semen on the backs of lovers of pointless one-night stands; of lubricants in the vagina of an eternally sad woman; of red wine dripping down the breasts of a woman in a hotel close to the Paseo de la Reforma. Tattoo or scar of a woman I met in a bar, of ten women I met in ten bars and loved me in the motels of drunkenness. Tattoo or scar of faked orgasms, of condoms strewn on the floor, of beer, of exchanged telephone numbers in fleeting napkins. Anyone will do, could be you. Sexual scar. Scar of the solitude of the end of the century. Let me be your love. Let me be your tattoo.

MEXICAN-STYLE LOVE? Why should it be different from other foreign loves? Constancia and I drank our coffee in Coyoacán and then went for a slow walk, stopping occasionally to admire some of my favorite façades. Later we entered the bar of a restaurant in Altavista Avenue while the signs of seduction manifested themselves, took a more defined shape. A way of stopping one's eyes in the eyes of the other, a tense silence of eternal seconds, broken by a smile.

Constancia was divorced and had two daughters. Her ex-husband was an industrialist from Monterrey, one of those rich men with a pedigree, and she herself was part of a prominent family from Nuevo León. Constancia was in the process of moving to Mexico City as the result of a decision that had to do with her interior need to put miles between her prior life and her recent freedom. Also, she had decided to paint more seriously. After her divorce Monterrey became too small for her.

Constancia was a little over thirty and some of our experiences from childhood and adolescence were similar.

We had watched the same television shows, listened to the same songs on the radio, seen the same movies of Jorge Negrete and Tin-Tan. We had read La Familia Burrón, had eaten Kellogg's Corn Flakes for breakfast, and sung the same national anthem in school. Our communication was possible because there was a code of similar cultures. To me this was totally new and extremely enjoyable. Japanese, Russian, Swedish, French, Italian, Irish, black, yellow, and white Americans, Brazilians, and even Spanish girls had not been able to give me this. I had been incapable of giving them anything other than the amazement of discovering the things we had in common despite the great differences. And Constancia used Spanish beautifully, without any fear, with absolute security. She also had a filthy mouth; perhaps because she had always been an upper class girl, a rich girl, and speaking like a rude cowboy had always been the privilege of upper class Mexican women. That night we laughed a lot and this is always a good sign.

People looked at us with curiosity. We both were dressed in black and there was something in our attitude that made it clear that we were not locals. Also, Constancia's beauty was notable. A beauty made of contrasts: green eyes and black hair. A South of the Border Bettie Page with a body she did not try to hide, but rather emphasized, without inhibitions, the cleavage of her black dress, its tight and elegant cut, the long legs, pale, without stockings. An assured beauty, definitely rare in a city where the immense majority of women do not know how to dress or wear makeup.

Since she was able to afford it, Constancia went to New York at least once a year to visit galleries, to buy clothes in Chelsea and Soho, to forget about Mexico and her everyday life. When she told me that Mexico sometimes seemed small to her I understood what she was trying to tell me. I remembered something that had to do with my own relationship with our country: Mexico lacked sensuality. Everything in her attitude towards life—and towards me—made sense. Constancia had married someone much older when she was very young. She now felt terribly unsatisfied for not having ever enjoyed a completely independent life. Her beauty and her last name were mere assets in the capital of a husband who had drifted apart from her over the years.

Constancia, finding you was my Mexican reward for all the rebuffs I suffered during my teenage years. All those young women, who were beautiful and arrogant back then, are now housewives with two or three noisy brats, poorly tinted gray hairs, and overweight husbands who probably spend most of their time in front of the television. Women I used to love and live now with the greater part of their dreams broken in pieces.

We went to her hotel. I didn't have to insinuate anything. For the first time a Mexican woman wouldn't waste our time on stupid games. I didn't have to belittle myself or lose my dignity. I asked her where she was staying and she mentioned the name of some hotel on Paseo de la Reforma. I asked her if, from her room, she could see the Angel of Independence, the statue that stands on an obelisque and tends to take a dive every time there is a major earthquake. She said she could. "I would love to see it from your window," I said. "And I would love to show it to you," she replied looking into my eyes. I kissed her hand again and almost in silence we drove downtown in her rented car listening to a Luis Miguel tape, of whom Constancia said, "Oh my god, he is so fucking hot," as I simply smiled as I never had in my lost hometown.

"CONSTANCIA, when did you decide this would happen?"

"I think as soon as you walked into Alberto's house. One always knows."

I am sitting on a chair. My left elbow is resting on the surface of a dresser. On the dresser there is a bottle of Portuguese wine we bought on the way to the hotel and an ashtray with two lit cigarettes. Straddled over me, naked, Constancia caresses my hair. The index finger of my right hand draws circles on her left breast; leaves it to caress her shoulder, comes down drawing lines in between the freckles of her chest, traveling the outline of that hard, erect tit, already swollen from kisses and tender bites. We are drinking and we still haven't fucked.

"Are you always this honest with yourself when you decide who you are going to sleep with?"

"No, but in your case I made an exception."

I dip that same index finger into my wineglass and now the drawing leaves a trace of small burgundy-colored pearls. Constancia looks at me fixedly in the eyes. My left hand takes her cigarette and puts it to her lips. Constancia

67

inhales. I leave the cigarette on the ashtray and my hand goes down her back feeling the bones of the spine of this woman who now exhales the smoke through her mouth while she lets me do what I wish with her body. I sink my hand between her buttocks and in that instant I realize what I am doing. I look at myself from the outside and I like what I see.

"I had never been like this before, naked on top of someone, without making love, just talking."

"Most guys think that sex is just fucking. For me penetrating a woman is not as important as it is for other men..."

Constancia doesn't say anything. She closes her eyes and smells my skin.

"And you, what do you look for when you make love?"

"Me? I guess I look for intimacy. To be loved, I suppose."

Constancia moves her hand towards where my hand explores the cleft of her ass and she caresses the skin of my testicles with her nails. With the other hand she takes one of the glasses and makes me drink, guessing that once again my throat is dry. I drink half of the wine I have in my mouth and make a gesture towards hers. Constancia passes her tongue over her lips and gives them to me. The wine begins to flow from one mouth to the other; our tongues stir it as if trying to create a little storm in a dark and tepid sea, a lascivious, newborn sea. She decides to drink the sea in a single swallow. A drop slides shyly toward her chin and I lick it.

She looks at me from the mirror on the large dresser.

I don't know which one I like more, the one who looks at me from the quicksilver distance or the one I have sitting on top of me, I tell her. She responds by taking my cock in her hand and making a hip movement to put it in herself while her eyes close and I look alternately at the two faces, still undecided.

MILAN KUNDERA'S SEDUCER in *The Unbearable Lightness of Being*, Tomas, is a modern Don Juan confused between two worlds that reflect each other in a distorted way. One is the world of pure desire and the other that of contaminated desire. The world of pure desire is the world of erotic, intellectual desire. The world of contaminated desire is the world of pornography. In this world sex has more to do with the exercise of masculine power. As a rule, this power seeks mostly total acceptance and absolute submission. In this world there is no perception of a woman as an equal, as part of a pair, someone who has the same desires and rights. The attraction Tomas experiences for the women he meets along the way in Kundera's novel and his need to establish "erotic friendships" with them is an almost childish attraction because it lacks some degree of perversion. Nothing wrong with this, Kundera's seducer is a product of Eastern Europe, provincial and economically relegated. Tomas is a Third World seducer, like a Latin American seducer would be.

In a brief and memorable essay the Argentine writer Julio

Cortázar complained about the scarcity of erotic themes in Latin American literature. For him, all that had been written in this genre, in the portion that corresponded to the Spanish speakers on our continent, seemed to be irremediably soaked with sexual fluids and full of pubic hairs. For him there was a delicacy missing which distinguishes the erotic from the pornographic in those sticky pages. The tension which makes these two energies move, almost always in opposite directions, has a different origin in each case. The erotic emerges from the intellect, not the spontaneous physical urge —that is, however, what the theorists and priests of good taste want us to believe: the truth is that eroticism is as well the tamed, castrated pornography of the bourgeoisie.

The end of these times is eminently pornographic. But perhaps it is not the end, but the beginning, and our pleas will be the echo of the winds that howl their prophetic solitude in the desert.

"I AM HUNGRY."

Constancia, naked on the bed, was looking at the ceiling or at the smoke of her cigarette that floated next to it. We had spent over a week making love to each other, fucking. I would leave to attend to my few commitments in the city while she shopped and visited galleries.

I, sitting once again on the chair drinking my red wine, was watching her. It seemed impossible that a woman almost my age, with two daughters, could have this body, I would tell myself, in total disbelief. I asked her what she wanted to eat, where she wanted to go. Too many years had passed since I had experienced the city on a daily basis and I could not think of any restaurants. But Constancia, like all the women I have dealt with in my life, delegated upon me the responsibility of choosing a place to have dinner. I decided that we would go to the Colonia Condesa.

Of all the neighborhoods of the city, Hipódromo Condesa is my favorite. The image that I have of Mexico City when I am abroad is not that of the neighborhood in which I grew up, nor the most important streets, avenues or landmarks of the city. I evoke Mexico City through the image of the Parque España and the Parque México; the restaurants of the Avenida Amsterdam, the Condesa Buildings, the boulevard of Avenida Mazatlán. La Condesa is a barrio of writers and poets, of musicians and artists; but also of underpaid maids, of sidewalks covered in dog shit, bourgeois people in all shapes and sizes who share that bohemian space in a harmonious manner. A kind of Greenwich Village or North Beach or Recoleta in the middle of a dying city.

We arrived and found parking easily. We walked by Amsterdam Avenue looking for a place to eat that was not too big. We immediately scratched the idea of going to Seps because of its decadent cantina style. Nothing Argentinean, please, I asked Constancia, it's usually expensive and bad, I explained. We found El Principio. We were welcomed by the hostess and immediately felt like the few people dining there examined us with discreet curiosity.

"It must be obvious that we are not from around here," Constancia said.

"Yeah, hell, it happens to me all the time," I replied. "When you leave your country you no longer belong to any place. In the United States it is impossible for me to feel at home, I will always be a foreigner even if I stay there for the rest of my life. Here it is the same thing: you leave and it is as if leaving in the middle of a movie; when you come back into the theater you no longer understand what the hell is going on, you have to ask for explanations that people are just too lazy to give you. Yesterday a taxi driver asked me where I was from. I told him I was a local to get him off my back and he laughed, he said it wasn't true, that I must be South American on account of my accent. My accent, give me a break…"

"That is so true… It happens to me too. The worst is when some jerk comes up to me and starts to speak to me in English. I answer them first in French and then when they look like they don't have a clue, I laugh in their face and in straight Monterrey accent I tell them to fuck off."

The waiter came by to take our order and I asked for a bottle of Chilean wine and bread, for starters. We lit up our cigarettes and a couple of Americans seated next to us said in English that Mexicans were an uncivilized people because we even smoked in hospitals. Just what I needed. It was bad enough that the fucking American laws had denied us smokers the right to smoke in any public place in California, but to come here and put up with the same puritan attitude in my own city was just to much.

"It really pisses me off that when tourists go to Rome they just won't behave as Romans do, and on top of it they complain," I said in English.

"Absolutely, I could not agree more," Constancia answered. Her accent was impeccable.

The Americans sunk into their plates and didn't even turn to look at us, probably embarrassed.

We immediately forgot about them.

"What are we going to do?" Constancia asked me, taking my left hand and putting it up to her mouth to kiss it.

"Anything, as long as we see each other as often as possible."

I kissed her hand, asking myself why women kissed men's hands so much.

"I am going to visit you. I won't be able to stand more than two months without you, you jerk. You haven't even left yet and I am already upset just thinking about how much I am going to miss you. Why the hell do you have to live in California?"

"And what about you? Why the hell do you live in Monterrey? What is there in Monterrey that you can't find here or in San Francisco?"

"You dumb fuck. All I am saying is that it is going to be a bitch when you leave, pendejo."

The expression on her face was delicious when she spoke like that, like a street vendor. I enjoyed people listening to us, because probably the people sitting around us were doing just that, even though Constancia and I didn't give a rat's ass because we were not from there. It was our city, but it wasn't. It was the city of my past and of her future, but in that moment made of kisses and red wine, Mexico City was entirely ours.

We ate and drank well. We left and sat in El Cafecito to drink an espresso and watched the other couples who came and went from the restaurants and shops.

"If you ever come back to Mexico," she said suddenly breaking the silence, "I don't want to live with you."

I felt relieved. I had already told her that I didn't want to get married or live with anyone. I still felt curious to know the motives of that spontaneous declaration.

"Because I don't want to impose my daughters upon anyone. They are mine and no one else's."

I lifted my coffee cup towards hers.

"Today I am going to give you head until you faint, my darling," I said with a dirty smile.

"I love you too."

She said this looking into my eyes so intensely that at that moment I felt sure that no one had ever loved me in that way before, and it would truly be a bitch if anyone were to do so in the future. Not like that, with that passion.

I didn't want to live with her either. I liked the idea of seeing her all the time, but I couldn't wake up by her side every day and see her with her hair in a mess and without makeup. One of Constancia's greatest attractions was precisely that perfection of image she worked on every day before leaving the house. She didn't have to do much because she was immensely beautiful. The care with which she outlined her eyes, her impeccable hairstyle, her clothes always elegant even in casual moments; it was all part of a spectacle in which I had a first row seat and exclusive backstage rights. I liked her like that. I didn't want her snoring by my side, drooling on the pillow, farting, sick, sweaty. Nor did she care to show me that perfectly human side of her. On the other hand, she was rich. She had always been rich and continued to be so after her divorce. Our situation, were we to live together, would be unbalanced, because even though I was not poor I could not live up to that level of circumstances. And then there were her daughters. I would never consider becoming a stepfather just as I had never considered becoming a father. Either she knew this or sensed it, and the arrangement was perfect for both of us.

We left the cafe and walked around the streets of La Colonia Condesa hand in hand until we decided to go back to her hotel. I was leaving the next day and our bodies had several pending issues before the separation.

When we reached the room we no longer spoke, or rather we spoke that other language where words are no longer necessary. Language of kisses on the surface of the water. Tattoo of sentimental ink upon her body.

I don't remember exactly at what moment of the night I took a pen from the writing desk and began writing words upon her breasts. The light friction of the point of the pen on her naked body gave her pleasure.

At first I wrote phrases from some of my favorite books; then lines from poems I remembered; then words that came from inside of me. Cover my body with words, she requested. Mark me. I don't know for how long I wrote my loving and fragmented discourse. But I covered her back and her breasts, her stomach, her ass and her thighs with words and words. I tattooed her with language and desire.

I couldn't part from her without leaving her something more than the memory of my body and my humid kisses. But words are not the patrimony of eternity. By the next day, when we awoke, I discovered that her skin had devoured the ink. There was no trace of what I had written. I smiled, thinking that all our efforts to last are useless just as the very impulse that precedes each one of them. I woke her with a kiss on the lips and she looked at me with her green liquid eyes.

"Make love to me before you leave." Her voice had the warmth of her gaze.

WHAT MAKES ME MEXICAN? My face? My name? My passport? Some years ago I told a friend that I no longer wanted to be a Mexican. My friend looked at me with concern and said, "Watch out, you better be careful whom you say that kind of thing to." And of course I was. A little like in that poem by José Emilio Pacheco called "High Treason" which starts by asserting "I do not love my country," I don't love that idea of the country that has been sold to us in exchange for our taxes, our puerile salaries, our violated votes. I am tired of seeing gigantic flags that wave with absurd and laughable pride, when I realize that while we fill ourselves with ecstasy in contemplation of the flag, they screw us with another WalMart, another concession, another franchise, another piece of foreign flesh busting the ass off our nationalism without us seeming to notice.

And also, what does it mean to be Mexican in a foreign land? I speak only from my own experience. Each time I eat at a restaurant in San Francisco I see those dark Mexican faces peaking timidly from the kitchens and that presence of servitude of my countrymen hurts me. I see the dishwashers, the domestic help, the nannies; I see from the highway that crosses the Californian Central Valley the hundreds of farmhands who collect the fruits and vegetables we buy in the fancy supermarkets; I see the day laborers of the Mission District who wait on César Chavez street for someone to hire them for at least a couple of hours; I see how California has turned them into its scapegoat, its enemy, its unwanted child. I am only a witness to all of this. My Mexican colleagues who teach at the American universities see another California. I have not been able to restrict myself to the campus. I never wanted to reduce my experience of this country to a cubicle, to a library. Following a woman's scent I found myself suddenly in the heart of the real life of California. There, in the middle of that difficult heart, I discovered that to be Mexican in California meant simply to be one more in a country of absolute anonymity. It meant nothing. I thought about this so as not to think about Constancia's mouth while the plane arrived at San Francisco.

MARIANNE INSISTED ON PICKING ME UP at the San Francisco airport the same way that Constancia had insisted on taking me to the one in Mexico. My body was red hot when I left Mexico and I had to make up an excuse so as not to submerge myself in Marianne's body the night of my return.

However, the following two weeks belonged to Sabine, since Marianne had received instructions from the London press for which she still worked as a freelancer to go to New Mexico to photograph some 18th century churches, and she left the day after my arrival. Sabine was happy to have her Mexican gentleman by her side once again but she was finalizing her plans for her return to Buenos Aires.

Sabine had spent six months in California and missed every aspect of her Buenos Aires. She found it obscene that *yanquis* dined at six o'clock in the afternoon, that bars and clubs closed at two, and that nobody spoke to each other on the streets; she thought it ridiculous that the city was deserted by nine at night, that the food was so fattening, that blacks and Mexicans were treated so badly, that people were so fat and ugly. In short, she was terribly offended by the fact that San Francisco was not Buenos Aires. She had managed to improve her English and it was time to return to her apartment in Belgrano, to her friends, to her adored cafes and bookstores that closed at five in the morning.

I was thoroughly entertained by being with her. She was a kid, amazed by everything, who spoke without stopping and sometimes asked the strangest questions. I have a surprise for you, she told me as soon as I met her at our favorite bar. Look. She lifted the hem of her jeans and showed me, very proudly, a tattoo that looked like a fine and delicate branch that went around her right ankle but that was also some sort of Arabic writing which I would never be able to read. "I love it," I said enthusiastically.

She was a kid. She was only twenty-three years old and her huge eyes denounced an innocence unknown to me. She was prettier than ever. She had dyed a tuft of hair with brilliant colors: blue, red, yellow, fuchsia and green in order to shock her parents and friends. Her impending return to Buenos Aires filled her with the energy of anticipation. She could not stop buying things, presents, souvenirs. One afternoon I had the unhappy idea of going shopping with her, and I saw her spend two thousand dollars in unexplainable objects. Electronic gadgets, makeup, a steam iron and deodorants for her father among other things. She was a kid with an inexhaustible credit card and no ideological problems with shopping.

And I spoiled her with loving words to which she listened with embarrassment, without knowing what to do or how to respond. Our physical surrender was more like an extension of our friendship. She was beautiful as only Argentinean women can be. However, her plane ticket was a clear sign that any attempt to try to stop her made little sense. She would leave and we would not see each other again. Those last two weeks were so sweet that the pain of my recent separation from Constancia gradually got numb. My constant telephone calls to Monterrey, where she had returned, and hers to my apartment, belonged in an untouched territory where my memory of what I lived with her in that hotel belonged to another dimension. A dimension that had nothing to do with my North American reality. I was back with Sabine even though I had left my skin with Constancia. Marianne was so free that a couple of postcards and a few phone calls from Santa Fe were the absolute testimony of her commitment to our relationship. So all my spare time was for Sabine. A few days before leaving Sabine told me that she would have to go to a hotel because her apartment contract was up and she didn't want to pay more money for days she wouldn't be there. I offered her my space and after thinking about it carefully for about six seconds she simply said okay, amused by the idea of sleeping by my side for a few days.

They were days of great tenderness and occasional tears. She had never met a man who treated her like a woman. All her Argentinean boyfriends had been boys her age, insecure, inexperienced. I was about a dozen years older and treated her like my equal at every moment. I liked that contrast of ages and experiences and I told her so. She blushed. She came to my house with three huge suitcases that almost broke my back. Paying no attention to my caresses, she went to the kitchen looking for something she might prepare, hoping to please me with her cooking. Something domestic invaded my apartment. Her gaze traveled through my space and stopped in certain corners. "Here you need a stand for the stereo, come here, what do you think about putting some plants here. How is it possible that you have no curtains?" To suddenly have a twenty-three-year-old mother giving me orders made me extremely nervous, but I let her play housewife for a few days. The night before her departure something happened. I had gotten so used to her presence that I didn't want her to go back to her country. She cried in silence and it broke my heart to see her like that. She made me promise her two things. First, if I ever got married it would be to her; second, that I had to come see her in Buenos Aires so that she could show me her city, the way I had shown her my version of San Francisco, impossible to be discovered by tourists. I agreed. They were two petitions that, in that moment, I found delicious.

The shock of taking her to the airport and seeing her leave with her walkman in hand and her eyes full of tears as her rainbow of hair fell over her face was too painful to recall. I returned to my apartment and suddenly felt old and lonely.

SABINE, I RETURNED FROM THE AIRPORT and went through the house surprised that you were no longer with me.

For the first time my house was a space made up of echoes. The towel you had used to dry your hair was still damp and held the scent of your shampoo. The refrigerator was still full of your vegetables and your nonfat yogurts. The cats looked at me and in their eyes there was a question for which I had no answer.

Many years ago I had decided to never get married, not have children, not own a house. I liked the idea of a life without roots. Teaching, spending my salary on books and CDs and eating in restaurants with girlfriends made up my idea of a perfect life. You brought me a feeling of restlessness unknown until your arrival. You offered me your youth, your singular happiness full of energy, and projects impossible for me but totally achievable by your side. You offered me your unknown city. A Buenos Aires that was for me, a literary reference filled with echoes of hoarse bandoneones. I loved tango because my soul was nocturnal and tragic. I loved, even before knowing you, the streets where Bioy Casares and Borges carved in eternity their subsequent history. I loved the silences of Sabato sitting on the bench of his Parque Lezama waiting for the characters of his dark novels to go by. As soon as you left I decided that I would go look for you. I had to make you come back to this city that had brought us together because I felt empty that night upon returning. Like a vampire, I needed your young blood to survive the night of my erotic anxiety.

I had Marianne, but Marianne was like the air, nothing could contain her, she possessed a freedom I would never have, and she would never—even though she had come to me with her suitcases—resign herself to a sedentary life of coffee and newspaper every morning, vacations only during the summer. Like the air, she traveled the earth freely and in her eyes was registered what her photographs captured. Like the air, her essence was indefinition.

Constancia was like clean water that came to placate an old thirst. She was the return to an origin that had begun in the aquatic belly of my mother. Constancia came with her green eyes of water to let me drink my ration of fresh, intense, clean sex. It all began in the water, not on earth. And Constancia led me in a stream of quick minutes to that primary ocean where I re-encountered my Mexican face, my language, and my city. Her love was like the rain that cleans the streets of the very noble and mistreated Mexico City in August. And my body was a busy street, so dirty, spit upon, that only Constancia knew how to clean with her kisses of water.

And you Sabine, my third element, were the solidity of the Promised Land. You were the earth where my nomadic soul could stop searching in those bodies temporary refuge. Root of light. Wide fertile plane of true words. Furrow of small smiles. But I would have to go look for you.

CONSTANCIA,

I think about you with unusual constancy. I think about your sex and about your ass. I have that image of you sitting on top of me, not facing me like the first night, but rather with your back to me, while I am inside of you and what I see is your hair, your slender waist, your ass that becomes wide in that position, your ass the sight of which makes me unbearably horny. I see my hands grabbing your flesh, squeezing it with greed, running my fingers over your ass, and pulling you towards me to enter more deeply within you, so that my swollen cock will touch you in your deepest recesses. now that thanks to this desire my cock is hard, I would like to have you sitting on this chair, with your back towards me, and stick my cock in you very slowly while my hands caress your breasts once again and I kiss your neck as I whisper things into your ear: I want to corrupt you... I want to suck each hair of your pussy until I make you come... I want you to suck my cock and see the semen drip from the creases of your mouth and fall upon your tits... I want to fuck you and come inside of you until I am dry, and later I want you to make me hard again with your wise tongue and put it inside of you until it hurts us *both... I want to cover your tits and your buttocks with scented oil and stick a finger up your ass... I want to rape you, fuck you, feel you up, not respect a single one of your holes, not listen to your screams of pain or listen to them and get even hornier... I want to stick a couple of fingers in your pussy while I drive onAvenida Insurgentes and suck my fingers once again like I did that night... I want you to suck me while I drive... I want us to go dancing and you not to wear panties so I can finger you whenever I want to... I want you to run your tongue over my ass and have you rape me and do as you please with me... I want to bite your nipples and bite your ass and suck your vaginal lips until they are swollen... I want to once again, while you get dressed standing in front of a mirror before we leave, kneel behind you, spread open your legs and push aside your underwear to suck you while you watch yourself in the mirror and I sink my face in your pubic hair scented of hours of sex... I want to hold you by your hair while you lick me... I want to feel the smell of your pussy on my chin and my lips... I want us to do things we have not done yet... I want you to tell me how you want me to fuck you... I want to get you drunk, fuck you while you sleep, wake you with kisses at dawn, turn you over, open your legs, and enter you until you no longer know if you are dreaming or if you are awake while the only thing you hear is my whimpering as I spill myself in your insides... I want you to suck every inch of my hairy testicles and the veins of my cock... I want all of me to smell like your sweat, your saliva, your shampoo, your perfume, your cum... I want you to scratch my back, to bury your nails in me while you come... I want you to squeeze me between your legs and not let me go from them until the century has ended... I want you to come in my mouth... I want to open your vaginal lips kneeling in front of you and put only the tip of my cock into you for eternal minutes until you go mad and force me to enter and I reach that point of no return... I want to kiss you and see your eyes while you blush and tears of happiness roll down your cheeks in the exact instant in which I fill you with my caring, warm, loving semen.*

SWEET DREAMS ARE MADE OF THIS. After seeing an irrelevant movie I got into my car to go back to my apartment. Halfway there I decided that it was too early to go back home—what would I do alone in that cage of my instinct?—so I headed to the studio of my painter friend. Gustavo has one of the best studios on Folsom Street in the Soma District. Soma is to San Francisco what Soho is to New York, with the difference that is not as trendy. A few galleries, gay and straight bars, cafes, clubs, people dressed in black at all times of day. It is always a problem to find parking in this fucking city; that is why I had to leave my car three blocks from the studio. It was only Wednesday yet the pre-weekend craze had already begun. Bars were full of women and more women in groups of two or three. The scarcity of men is notorious in this city where according to my single girlfriends most of the men are either gay or are tough macho types. That night there was something in the coldish air of San Francisco, not only that peculiar vibration that refined cities always have at the beginning of the weekend, but something else. I arrived at his studio and found Gustavo drinking wine by himself. It was a bottle of one of those fancy Californian wines that we simple mortals cannot afford. He was still in his work clothes and was sitting in front of one of those huge paintings that only he knows how to paint. A CD of Nusrat Fateh Ali Khan blasted through the speakers to counteract the sound of the jukebox of El Bobo, the bar two stories down. Since the buildings of California are made of wood, and not concrete and brick, they allow for even the most indiscreet sounds to filter through its walls. "What's up professor, you want a little wine?" We drank what was left in the bottle and Gustavo brought out another. "This one," he said, "was given to me by a friend; it is a Sonoma Merlot. Let's see how good it is." We talked about painting, about people we both knew, women, Mexican politics. It got late and I decided to leave. I left the studio and the sight of the full moon stopped me. The moon, I told myself, that explains this weird feeling, this call of the city. I started to walk back to my car and when I turned a corner I came upon a group of six or seven guys and girls.

They all were dressed in black. Some had capes, most of them wore velvet clothing, silver-studded black leather chokers, nose rings, eyebrow rings, lip rings. Their faces were covered with white makeup. Their hair—probably blond—was dyed jet black, their fingernails and their mouths painted black. The women wore very tight clothes, some had corsets, black ribbons, lace, garters, high-heeled stilettos, high boots, and the contrast of all that black with their pale flesh was too much temptation. I followed them with my eyes while I lit a cigarette. I saw them stop at the door of a club. TROCADERO, read the discreet sign. I approached the entrance of the club. I pushed aside the red velvet curtain that blocked the view from the street and three young kids dressed in the same manner as the others looked at me. "What is going on here tonight?" "Industrial music, Goth stuff, anything," they said. I paid the fifteen-dollar cover charge that those of us who were not appropriately dressed had to pay. I was dressed in black as usual, well dressed, but definitely not like a vampire. The song playing at full volume was perfectly appropriate for the scene that my eyes discovered.

In the basement towards which the stairs led me there were about fifty vampires. I remembered the novels by Anne Rice, *Interview with the Vampire* and *The Vampire Lestat.* As I cautiously advanced in the dark hallway some of them looked at me from head to toe, but most of them ignored me. After all, a cat is very much like a vampire, I thought. I went up to the bar and asked for a martini. The bartender looked at me as if I had asked for the telephone to call Madonna. Only beer and wine, he informed me impatiently. Beer. Anchor Steam. I paid the four dollars with a five and the bartender assumed correctly that the change was for him even though I had not made it obvious yet. I turned around with my beer in hand and with my eyes I scoured, no, I licked the human landscape. By my side there was a young lady of about twenty who had her white breasts exposed and her nipples covered with little black cones made of satin. She turned and said cheers in Italian. I lifted my drink like a gentleman, said cheers in Spanish and turned again to begin exploring the place. I discovered a hallway where there were more vampires sitting and talking in a lively way. The music was interesting and even though it flooded the space with its obsessive rhythm it was not deafening like in most clubs. Well, I said to myself, these people seem to enjoy conversation.

The hallway took me to the main floor of the club where some kind of performance was coming to an end. A huge metal frame held the body of a semi-naked male who was being symbolically whipped by a dominatrix with an imposing body. In the air there was a smell of sex and humidity that began to disturb me. Some three or four girls danced a kind of ritual dance to the rhythm of a song that mixed Gregorian chants with synthesizers. I took a long drink of my beer and lit another cigarette. The quasi-sado-masochistic vampires finished their act and pleased with themselves, they thanked the applause of their public. Next, the DJ played a song that had to be very popular in the vampire community because the dance floor filled right away. The style of dance was sensual and harmonious. Almost no one danced with a partner. Men and women danced on their own and those of us not dancing observed with interest the bodies on the dance floor. Dry ice, purple lighting, a subtle aroma of incense and sweat. I thought that the place was very much like an impossible church. The women were beyond beautiful. Some made believe they were some sort of gothic priestess, others had chosen bondage clothing made of vinyl and black leather, others simply looked like daughters of the night whose full moon made it possible for the tension reigning in the club to penetrate each pore of the skin. I drank the rest of my beer and returned to the bar for another.

The skin is sensitive to the gaze.

I saw her leaning up against the bar, all by herself. Her back had a tattoo on the right shoulder blade. It was a Miró cat if the Catalan painter ever painted a cat. The bartender was ignoring me but suddenly the beer had no importance whatsoever. The cat fixed its eyes on me. My eyes returned the stare and I could see how the cat shivered. I stared at it with intensity. Stupid cat, I thought to myself, don't fuck with me. The cat returned a glance that was difficult to sustain. They were a pair of yellow, piercing eyes. I liked that duel because it was taking place on a soft territory and I guessed that in the pores of the skin of the cat, in the pores of the skin of that soft shoulder blade, there was a movement of cells and blood that called to me, that reacted to my insolent stare at that epidermis I wanted to touch. The cat may have guessed my intentions and closed its eyes slowly. It moved its skin with a particular quiver, as if to keep something unknown from touching it, or as if it had felt a sudden fear which it was not willing to acknowledge as such, and decided to do a one hundred and eighty degree turn. The owner of the cat looked at me and said, "Do you like my pussy?" Voice and eyes were the same thing.

"I don't know yet," I answered.

"I felt your gaze. Did you like my cat?" she insisted.

"I am not always responsible for what my eyes like," I smiled.

"Cats ignore all sense of responsibility. Also," she continued with that tyrant voice, "cat's eyes are, of all the signs on earth, the most equivocal and indecipherable." She smiled before taking a sip from her glass of red wine.

I laughed and said that there was no indecipherable sign, that the only indecipherable thing was the stupidity of the readers of signs.

"How old are you?" she asked.

"Thirty-five."

I took a cigarette pack out of the pocket of my jacket and offered her one before taking mine. She took one with her long black nails and placing it between her ring and middle fingers of her left hand she waited for me to take mine and light hers. *Sweet dreams are made of this. Some of them want to use you. Some of them want to be used by you.*

"Don't you want to know my age?"

"Does it matter?" I answered.

"Everything matters."

"OK... How old are you, kitty?"

"I have no age."

"But to get in here you have to show some sort of ID that proves that you are over twenty-one, right?"

"That doesn't mean anything." She looked at me through her wine glass.

"Do you know why I liked your cat?"

"Why?"

"Because it felt my glance."

She smiled, this time with a twisted gesture, but seemed to be pleased.

"That is why I am talking to you."

"I know." I took a deep breath.

We remained standing by the bar. Her cleavage evidenced a Miracle Bra for which I was thankful. Over the course of an hour, and two additional drinks each, we talked about panthers, about William Blake, cannibalism, satanic rituals, voodoo, bullfights, and labyrinths.

Suddenly she heard something that made her bring her head up, much like the way in which cats react to sounds impossible to hear for humans, and said to me "I love this song." She was going to dance and invited me not to dance with her but to watch her.

"Watch you?"

"Yes. Follow me."

On the dance floor she mixed herself in among the vampires. No. She couldn't mix in. She was different. She had a demeanor and a presence that distinguished her from those who occupied the dance floor. I became aware of this right away and for some reason, which I did not understand that very moment, I felt alarmed.

The gothic dance is a ritual that does not require partners. But she was the soloist of that vampire dance company. Those who, like myself, were aware of her movements watched her discreetly, even though one of the rules of the place seemed to be that of ignoring others; that was why the looks were oblique. I, who did not belong in the black velvet tribe, found myself thoroughly examining, without any hint of guilt, each muscle, each shadow of her body, each expression of her face, each lightning of violet light falling over her skin.

She danced for ten minutes and when the song was over she looked at me fixedly for a couple of seconds and turned around walking away toward the exit. I quickly went up to the DJ who was behind me and asked him the name of the band that played that obsessive song. "Crash Worship," he said.

I went to get another beer and saw her as she asked for her leather jacket at the coat check. Then she went up the stairs. I didn't follow her. But as soon as I lit another cigarette I felt the most horrible sadness. I felt like going outside to howl my pain under the moonlight. All night I felt I had no right to ask her for anything, not even her name.

AGONY IS SWEET IN THIS PIT.

In his beautiful essay entitled "The Sense of Beauty," based on the lectures he offered at Harvard a hundred years ago, the philosopher George Santayana writes about the "lower senses." These are the senses which "our" Western Christian civilization has traditionally considered as secondary. Until Santayana the senses of touch, taste, and smell had been called unaesthetic or non-aesthetic. Curiously these are the sexual senses par excellance. Maybe our culture had been so fearful of our sexuality that it had chosen to hierarchize the senses in that bigoted way. In the pit of sexuality the lower senses are at the deepest bottom and take us through secret tunnels to regions of unsuspected pleasure.

Traditionally the pit is a metaphor for the occult, just as the labyrinth is a metaphor for the indecipherable. The knowledge of the pit, coming into its darkness, implies a descent or a fall on our part, but the labyrinth requires an entrance. The pit is vertical; the labyrinth is horizontal. Like heaven and hell, like good and evil, the pit represents two opposite poles. The labyrinth does not, the labyrinth is a spiral in the shape of an interrogation, it is an enigma, a mystery. The labyrinth is a baroque question mark, it is the excess of doubt. The pit can be the result of a geological accident or of a man-made excavation, but the labyrinth is always artificial, it is born of desire. It is born of the genius of an architect, Daedalus, who is instructed by his queen, Pasiphaë, to build a structure that can hide the fruit of her perverse, bestial love.

Pasiphaë falls in love with a bull. Her passion for this formidable animal is such that she comes up with a plan: she isolates the bull and personally chooses a young cow from her herds which she places in a pen, near but inaccessible to the bull. The heifer arouses in the stud a sexual urgency that begins to drive it crazy. When the bull can no longer take it, Pasiphaë orders Daedalus to design a hollow frame that reproduces the shape of the heifer so that she can go inside. Once in she places herself in such a way that the bull can penetrate her. Next she has the heifer killed and the still warm skin of the animal is placed over the frame, which simulates it. She orders the barrier between the pens be removed and the crazed bull enters and mounts her, hidden and in heat under that bleeding skin.

This is how the minotaur Asterius is conceived, son of bestial passion and simulacrum. Daedalus then constructs, by order of the queen, the labyrinth, house of shame, dwelling of the Minotaur, horizontal spiral of terror, live metaphor of our times that represents, but also hides as an aberration, like the howl of Pasiphaë upon receiving the bull, our most prohibited, most secret desires.

In the center of his labyrinth a man digs a pit.

WHAT DID NARCISSUS AND HIS SISTER hunt in the woods? My sisters, dark like myself, also go out hunting in the forests of the night. Lunar Amazons. Seeing them in black I asked myself whether they were also in mourning. Widows of what deception, of what unfound answer? That is why the answer of the nameless woman surprised me so much when I found her again in that club. I had gone to look for her at the Trocadero and she was alone with her red wine and all that black silk.

"I am hunting," she said.

The Miró cat did not look at me: it slept hidden on her back.

"I need to know your name," I said. She looked at me amused.

"I think today my name should be that of a queen, since I feel particularly inclined to be arrogant, and to be served."

"Fuck you," I told her. "I like the fact that you have an attitude, but I will not serve you."

Placing herself in front of me she put one hand on my

nape and began burying her long black painted nails into the skin of my neck. I did not protest. She brought me towards her mouth and kissed me and while she did that she continued to sink her nails into me. It was a deep kiss, not quite intimate, made up of tongue and nothing else. Suddenly she bit my lips and I pushed her away taking hold of her shoulders. I thought I had discovered the game and I simply said no, but with a gesture that explained that I did not like the idea of a dominatrix, that I would never accept the pain of my body nor humiliation as a way to pleasure. She looked into my eyes fixedly and took a slow drink from her wineglass.

"You don't understand shit... I like men to dominate me, submit me, make love to me violently, fuck me, bite me, and bury their hard meat and their fingernails into me. For me, to serve me means to use me."

As I listened to these words I felt a knot in my throat and a warm feeling creating a sensation of pleasing asphyxiation. She looked at me and stroked the collar of my jacket with her nails.

"What is your name?" I asked her again.

"Justine... Juliette... whatever you like, it is all the same since I do not have a name."

I brought my right hand to her back and looked for an opening in her blouse. When I found it I began searching with my fingers the skin of her lower back and slowly buried my fingernails into that warm hidden skin while she initiated a waving movement with her shoulders and her waist like a fucking cat, like a cat in heat. I liked that reaction. I liked having come upon without notice into that unknown territory. I liked the idea of being able to be violent and having a woman like this at my mercy, to bite down hard on her nipples, burying my teeth on her buttocks, or whatever may come. I liked the possibility of not being me, or perhaps discovering an unknown me like the one who began to emerge from under my skin next to that new heat. For a fraction of a second I was afraid, but my curiosity was much stronger. Continuing with my nails on the prohibited journey, I remembered that old saying about curiosity and the cat, but I decided that the purring of the Miró cat was stronger than any sense of prudence. As she moved in that almost obscene way—shoulders and waist as if the cat on her back had completely overtaken her—I buried my nails into her and felt how they entered her skin. Then she came close to my ear and purred, "Fuck me."

I fell into the pit.

I DIDN'T KNOW HER NAME BUT I WAS IN HER APARTMENT.

As I drove toward Fillmore Street, where she lived, I had felt her gaze going over every inch of the skin of my face. Each time that I turned to look at her, I met eyes that were like two coals and it was difficult for me to confront them. I had to drive the car and that was enough of an excuse for my eyes not to stand in dignified battle with hers. I parked the car and followed her to the Victorian building where she lived.

As soon as we opened the door to her apartment she sprang upon me and began kissing me. She unzipped my pants while I lifted her blouse and pulled down her bra to leave her tits exposed. They were big and had small soft nipples that contrasted with the size of the rest of her breasts. I caressed them while she took my erect cock in her right hand. Suddenly she let go and told me to follow her. I followed her down a dark hallway and as she went into the bathroom she told me that if I wanted wine or beer to go to the kitchen. Fixing my pants I asked if I could smoke. I lit a cigarette next to the bathroom and began to listen to the powerful stream of her urine falling in the water of the toilet. I stayed for a moment next to the bathroom door remembering the "Widower's Tango" by Neruda and trying to hear the peculiar sound that toilet paper makes when it is rubbed against a vulva. I heard nothing other than the sound of the water taking away her warm urine to the depths of the pipes under the city.

She caught up to me in the kitchen and took out two wineglasses from a Mexican cabinet. She took out a bottle of Italian wine from a shelf and gave it to me to open along with a corkscrew that was on a table. I served the wine.

"Come," she said.

I followed her to the living room. She put on a CD and asked me if I knew the band.

"The Cure, right?"

I sat and she came to sit by my side.

"What do you want to do?" she asked.

"I want you to tell me your name."

"Today my name is Vida. It means life in Spanish. Why this obsession with names?"

"And what do you want to do?" I looked at her body with greed and ignored her question.

"I want us to drink this bottle of wine and then another. I want to listen to my favorite music. I want to show you my collection of lingerie."

"Are you going to model for my exclusive pleasure?" I asked her smiling.

"I model to earn my living, I could do it for you tonight."

At last she said something about her life. I was taken by the thought of being with a model and smiled. I had never had that much luck as a consumer and suddenly saw her in a new light. I understood why she was a model. In fact, now that she said it, I could not believe, even if she had told me so, that she had any other occupation.

"OK," I said. "Do it. Model."

She smiled as she stood up and started dancing to the rhythm of the music. Fucking bitch, I thought as she unbuttoned her blouse and uncovered her pale skin. She wore a long velvet skirt that came to her ankles, as she pushed it down over her hips she used the other hand to lift off her blouse. It was a wonderful vision, straight out of a noir erotic film. She had on a purple satin bra embroidered with black velvet, thong underwear, buried in her round, perfect ass, where she had tattooed a small labyrinth on the top of her right buttock. She danced as she had danced among the vampires the night I discovered her in the Trocadero. Like that night I watched her dance with greedy eyes. I licked her ephemeral and beautiful flesh with my gaze. I desired her without reservation and when the song was over I ordered her to take off her bra. She looked at me and took her hands to her back while I started to understand the rules of the dark game.

Her breasts lit up the night. She would stop for a few seconds to take sips from her glass and continued the dance. Her breasts were firm, young, almost adolescent. I drank and licked my lips. I lit a cigarette and when she stood on her toes with her back towards me, I reached out with my hand and grabbed her cunt as if I were taking an apple from a lubricious tree near me. I brought her towards me and on the sofa I discovered myself as dark as I had never been and wearing an unknown skin.

MY FINGERS SMELL OF VAGINA. I have so many images in my mind that they are all spliced together and do not allow me to give them individual identity. Our mouths intertwined, snatching each other's tongues. Bitten lips. Her nipples swollen and marked by my teeth. The flesh around her nipples reddish and probably turning purple by now. The middle finger of my right hand buried completely in her tiny clean asshole. I dug my fingernails into her back, into her arms, into her ass. My hands pressing the bones of her skull and filling themselves of that smell of smoke that I had never felt in the hair of any woman.

It is the morning of the next day and I am back at my house. I remember what happened and my body reacts with violence. I want more, fucking Jesus, I want more.

The phone rings; it is Marianne.

It is the second call this week but today she notices something strange in me, I am sort of distracted, she says.

She will arrive on Sunday. United. Flight 152. At 4:35 P.M.

She wants to have my children.

But she will never have them.
I am no longer afraid.
I want to go back to the brocade and the howling.

MARIANNE, TATTOOED WITH A PANTHER, and the nameless woman, tattooed with cat and labyrinth, were the two exemplary and opposite extremes of an old and tired civilization. Two extreme points which had touched through me.

In Marianne, the European world had birthed one of its most interesting manifestations. She was a young woman who looked to other cultures for signs of identity her eyes could translate to the common language of sight. Her photographs were respectful testimonies of unique moments. Her gaze was not that of the imperial kind, that of the anthropologist who travels like an Indiana Jones from Western culture to exotic lands looking for the last vestiges of the noble savage to report his findings in the *National Geographic*. Marianne was truly like the air that travels the surface of the earth and has no nationality nor makes distinctions among races or languages. Without religion, without fear, without prejudices, Marianne lived in the voyage, like a female Ulysses. But her Ithaca was the voyage itself.

The nameless woman was the perverse expression of that same culture's obscure side. An effeted, tired culture. Her violence was intellectual. Her bookshelves were filled with gothic literature and the works of Sade, Bataille, and Klossowski. All the authors published by Velvet, in London: Pantziarka, Krafft-Ebing, Whitehead, Jeremy Reed, Pierre Louÿs. There were books on tattoos, on sadomasochism, on vampires. But it was the poetry books that called my attention. She had a heterogeneous mix of poets from around the world. Books in French, in Italian, in Spanish. In her room nothing made too obvious her erotic preferences, but the half-opened closet revealed a collection of clothing that made me think of the closet of a true vampiress. Burgundy-colored brocades, black velvet, silk, satin, corsets, lace, all black, all soft to the touch, rough on the memory.

Her unpleasant, arrogant, and indifferent demeanor kept me intrigued. She was not interested in knowing anything specific about me. She was the selfishness of pleasure. She gave me everything that my body demanded of hers but any attempt at exchanging information on my part was reciprocated with an icy, artificial smile. A smile which said, "I don't give a damn what you think, what you want to know, what you are interested in." She was the feline par excellance. As such, she needed to be touched, manipulated, played with, but felt no obligation to give back anything other than her glance and the abandonment of her body. I felt in danger because as I began to understand what she demanded in silence, I liked the game even more. I found it captivating because it was unknown. From that understanding I realized that for the first time in my adult life I did not have control over anything, not even my body. I had been seduced.

The encounters succeeded each other with more frequency. Marianne had her own occupations and understood that I couldn't see her as she would have desired. I escaped to the Trocadero as often as I could and when I found the Countess (as I began to call her after our third or fourth encounter), sometimes in the arms of some beautiful, long-haired vampire, she would leave it all to come to me. She would kiss me and stay with me. Then we would go to her apartment where we would get drunk on red wine until that dark desire came back to take over our bodies. We would start to bite each other, to touch each other with violence, to look for something new to do so we would avoid boredom and predictability and eventually get fed up with the routine that takes over everything, even sex. But one day I found myself in love and I had to make a great effort to not let her know that. I knew that telling her would be the end, and my flesh could not afford that.

I tried to not look for her and to find refuge in Marianne, in my letters to Constancia, in my letters to Sabine. But one Saturday at two o'clock in the morning I saw myself leaving my house at top speed heading towards the club where she had told me she would be. After going through the place quickly I came to the conclusion that she was not there. It was too late to look for her in anoth-

113

er club so I drove to her house on Fillmore Street. Would I find the catwoman? Drawn by the yellow light in the window I saw two silhouettes. One of them was the Countess, the other silhouette was also that of a woman. They were kissing.

DENIS DE ROUGEMONT SAYS THAT WHAT TRULY EXALTS Western lyricism is not the pleasure of the senses nor "attained love," but rather our passion for love, and that this passion always means suffering. For that reason, to think about passion in the fabulous nineties reminds me of a song of Garbage, "#1 Crush," which, now that at the end of the century the idea of passion has changed so much, makes more sense than ever. I know it by heart:

> *I will care for you, feel pain for you*
> *I will twist a knife and bleed my aching heart*
> *and tear it apart*

After having taken the experience of love in this century to such extremes, what is left for us? In what terms can we define concepts such as passion itself, seduction, surrender? The form is the content: MTV, vampires, black clothing, tell me where you shop and I will tell you how much you owe, end-of-the-century anguish, decomposed philosophy, bondage, unilaterality, individualism, the absolute reign of the image, the death of sex, the death of the text; use me, kill me, bury your nails in me, I would steal for you, I would grovel at your feet, sell me your image or any image: anyone would do; the shape of your breasts mirrors the contents of your heart, your contact lenses are the window to your soul, you are what you appear to be, what you want me to believe that you are: the form is the content. Passion is nothing but the words that represent it. Use me. Dominate my instincts. I am empty: I am barely the silhouette of my appetite, a dark dance in an improbable place but true regardless of my eyes. Temple of dark love. Acid rain on the skin of decaying humanism. Untranslatable signs; the form is the content: we have finally arrived.

IN HIS *PERSIAN LETTERS*, published in 1721, Montesquieu says that the Persian women of that time not only expected their husbands to beat them, but moreover, they desired it. In order to support this terrible claim, he referred to the story of a common woman who wrote long letters to her friends complaining that her husband never beat her. Because of this lack of abuse her neighbors had started to talk behind her back. The absence of physical punishment was proof to them that her man did not love her. The woman swore in her letters that she tried in every way to provoke the wrath of her husband so that he would assault her. Faced with the futility of her efforts the woman came up with a private and disconcerting theater in the interior of the family home. Every night when her husband returned home the woman would start screaming and crying as if he were savagely beating her. When the husband tried to calm her by taking her by her shoulders, the woman would cry out in even more doleful screams, and thus she was finally able to convince her neighbors that her husband loved her above all things.

FOR THE ROMANTIC WHO WAS DYING WITHIN ME it was not easy to accept what the Countess expected, not only of me but also of any man or woman to whom she would offer herself: physical punishment as proof of love or acceptance. I had attended, with a certain degree of astonishment, the spectacle of myself doing things that I never imagined myself capable of doing.

One night, one dawn, I found myself doing something that alarmed me. I decided then that I had to do something to try to free myself from so much bittersweet darkness.

We had returned from a bar in Soma where alcohol and music had put us in a state of sordid drunkenness. The conversation at the bar had been along these lines:

"Why hadn't you told me that you slept with women?"

"You never asked me."

"The truth is that I like the idea, but for some reason it hadn't occurred to me that you might like to sleep with chicks."

"Yes, but, don't you think it makes sense, knowing me as you do?"

"The thing is that I don't know you, darling. Nor do you know me. Why do we fool ourselves with the illusion that we know each other?"

"You know more about me than most people will ever get to know."

"And what is it that I know about you? The way in which your tits get black and blue after I bite them for hours? That there is a barrier I cannot cross even though at the same time there are others, which most people almost never cross, that does not exist between us? You haven't even told me your name, you bitch Countess."

"Why the hell do you want to know my name? Don't you have enough with what I give you each time you come?"

"It isn't about that, I think you know what I am talking about."

"Look, you jerk, you better stick to drinking your wine and do me a favor."

"Whatever you please."

"Good. Listen to me: today I am not wearing any panties."

"Really?"

"Really. I want you to know that and to imagine my naked ass under my miniskirt. I am wearing a black garter and silk stockings that I bought especially for you. Tell me what you would do to me if at this moment I got up and went to the men's restroom and you were there with me, alone."

"Do you want me to tell you about it or do it to you?"

"For the moment just tell me about it."

I got up close to her ear and felt her thighs spreading to allow me to touch her. I slid my left hand under her skirt to confirm that in truth she was wearing no underwear. The contact of my fingers with her pubic hair and the vision of her evil smile made me swallow hard.

"I would close the door and then I'd slap you across the face."

"Why the slap?"

"For being a cunt. For going into the men's restroom without panties."

"OK. Go on."

"I'd tell you that you are a fucking whore and I'd slap you again."

"Again?"

"Again. For being a whore and for asking too many questions."

"OK," she exclaimed with a smile that was an amused protest. "And then what?"

"Then I'd kiss you on the mouth and order you to take off your blouse but not your bra. You'd look at me with resentment for having hit you and I'd tell you that if you look at me again like that I would knock your lights out for sure. You'd lower your eyes."

As I spoke I felt how the Countess reacted to my hand that moved slowly between her thighs. She was again swaying with that movement of her shoulders and her waist that since the first time I touched her would not stop haunting me whenever I was not by her side.

"Then I would order you to close your eyes and unzip my pants. You'd do it and I'd take you by your shoulders so I can see your face in the mirror, your eyes closing, your dark hair with its highlights and its smoky smell. I can almost see your breasts and through your transparent silk bra your small erect nipples."

"Like now. They are erect."

"Then I'd lift your miniskirt up to your waist and I'd see, I'd verify with my sight, what I now verify with my touch, that you are not wearing panties. In front of me, I have your white and round ass. The straps of the garter go down over them until they trap your new silk stockings and the contrast of your skin with the black garter, the way in which the stockings stretch over your thighs, and the dark shadow of your crack excites me."

"And what do I do?"

"You move your waist and your shoulders like you do now; like a panther in heat; like a vampiress who had in front of her the naked neck of a fourteen-year-old virgin; you move like the whore you are. Then I separate your legs with my knee..."

"That is enough."

"OK. What do you want to do?"

"I want to go to my castle."

"Rocking good news."

I took my hand out from in between her legs and sucked my fingers in an obscene fashion while I looked into her eyes. She took my fingers and put them into her mouth while I looked for the bartender with my eyes. I paid and we walked over to the car.

"Have you read *The Story of O?*" she asked without looking at me.

"Pauline Reage. I read it. Why?"

"Because now I want to play *The Story of O.*"

"Well... But you are missing the undies. On the other hand, you are already wearing the garter."

She lifted her skirt and put her naked ass down on the seat. Like the leading character of *The Story of O* she detailed for me the sensation of being seated on a leather seat without anything mediating between the skin of her ass and that of the seat. I smoked and listened to one of her Suzanne Vega tapes on the car stereo. I thought that it would have been interesting to submit her at that moment to an experiment, like in the novel, and take her to a place where a secret society of submissive women lived at the disposal of a bunch of fuckers who tortured them and used them as they pleased; but I was happy that our pleasure was private. After all I'm not French. I am Mexican.

We arrived at her apartment.

"Welcome to my estate."

"Thank you. Take your skirt off."

She took it off and then took her blouse off. Silk and velvet brocade. Garter and pubic hair. Pale jasmine skin like that of a neo-classical sculpture. She went to the kitchen to open a bottle of red wine while I went to pee in the bathroom. When I came out, she was leaning up against the wall next to the bathroom with a glass of wine in each hand and a dog collar around her neck. She was smiling. From the collar, studded with short spikes, hung a black leather leash that fell between her breasts and went down to her thighs. With one hand I took my glass of wine and with the other the leash. I swallowed the entire contents of the glass in one gulp and some drops leaked out the corners of my mouth.

"Lick these drops off me," I ordered her. She licked them.

We went into her room and I told her that I was going to hurt her and that there was nothing that she could do to stop it. Her slightly opened mouth, her fixed glance into my eyes and her anxious breath were proof that she cared about nothing other than our obscure session of rotten pleasure.

I pushed her down onto the bed and taking her by the waist I put her in front of me, kneeling with her back towards me. I put one finger in my mouth and I licked it. With the index finger and thumb of my left hand I separated her ass cheeks and after a few preparatory motions around that private skin I sunk my recently licked index finger into the naked ass she offered me. The Countess moaned as she followed the rhythm of my hand with her back and her shoulders.

For about two minutes I fingered her while I rested my wine glass on her back and smoked using her naked back as an ashtray to deposit the ashes of my cigarette. I was sinking my finger into her ass when a painful idea came to me. On my right there was a large dresser from where a lit candle witnessed the scene with its weak gaze. Without thinking I took it and rested the candleholder over her back. At first, I wanted light to be able to better watch my dirty and delicious task, but I remembered my readings of the divine Marquis. Perhaps the innocence of a spontaneous action would have saved me, but my literary background turned my action into something more perverse because of its premeditated nature. I remembered the story of Rose Keller and the trial which sent the Marquis de Sade to jail for the first time; I remembered the melted wax that the Marquis emptied over the open wounds of Rose Keller—wounds which he himself had inflicted on her in an atrocious kidnapping—and tilting the candle I began to slowly empty the drops of hot wax over the skin of the Countess' back. She reacted with a violent jerk to which I responded by holding her firmly by the neck with my free hand. When she turned she fixed her interrogative gaze into me and I responded by letting go of her neck only to sink my finger once again into the depths of her asshole. She emitted a weak complaint that I took advantage of by removing my finger and uniting the middle and index fingers in the penetration. I spat a wad of saliva on her anus to ease the entry and I took the candle once again leaning it over her lower back. I now had two fingers inside of her and several drops of dried wax as proof of my possession. Her garter, the naked nape of her neck, and the hoarse sound that came from her throat were the permission I needed to continue. I saw the collar and told myself that it was useless to think of anything. Everything in her was submission, permission to transgress, desire to cross sexual borders. I sunk the ring and little fingers into her vagina and I put the candle aside. With the left hand I held her by her hair.

"Tell me your name, you whore. Tell me your name. Tell me what you want from me."

Upon hearing this she became violently agitated and separated herself from me. With intense rage she looked at me through her violet eyes and told me to leave. I pushed her down onto the bed and threw myself on top of her. I took my cock in my hand and directed it towards that swollen and moist vulva that she was now denying me. She tried to reject me but I opened my way between her legs as she sunk her nails into my back and bit my right shoulder until it bled. I began to fuck her and when I was in the depths of her sex her bite became a moan of dirty pleasure, a howl of forbidden pleasure I can still hear. She kissed me and asked me to bite her, to break her bones, to not come and prolong her pleasure until she split in half and went mad.

I turned her and bent her over because the view of her ass was what excited me the most. I began to fuck her in the ass and she reacted with screams that were no longer of pain. She reached back and dug her fingernails into me; she bit any piece of skin that was at the reach of her mouth. I plunged my entire hand into her vagina. I bit her breasts until I drank a milk that was blood. We marked each other's backs with our fingernails and in them there were pieces of skin as trophies of a lubricious and forbidden war. I drank all of her, her blood, her vaginal juices, her saliva, her piss. I hit her, I insulted her, I fucked her again and again, and I could not contain her. She wanted more, she wanted something that I did not have and never would. My cock was falling apart in pieces and I could take it no longer. After an uncertain amount of time sleep won me over, but the hot mollusk that was her mouth woke me by licking my balls, sucking my cock hard once more. After that I tried to please her with my fingers, with my tongue, and I could not satiate the bitch in heat of her desire. I gave up. I was beat by the weakness of my legs and my disgust. Once again I sunk two fingers into her ass and two into her hungry vagina. I could not contain her.

The next day I decided to go south, the furthest possible south.

I CONTINUED TO LIE.

I invented a trip to a conference in Argentina so that Constancia would not come to see me in San Francisco. In our telephone conversations prior to my decision to go—fleeing is the privilege of the weak of flesh—to Buenos Aires, Constancia had announced that she was organizing her calendar to come to see me.

My relationship with the Countess was so sexual that I knew I would not be able to escape from her body to find refuge in Constancia's. I had marginalized Marianne as I fell deeper into the black pit that was the Countess' mind. As she was busy with her own projects, she did not demand very much of me. I was afraid of losing her, like I was afraid of losing Constancia and Sabine. But the Countess gave me no choice, only addiction to her perverse submissiveness.

One night I had dinner with Marianne and told her that I had to go on a trip. She did not know about my nightly whereabouts and understood that I needed to leave San Francisco for a couple of weeks. She could understand better than anyone the need to wake up the next day in a different place.

But Constancia was disappointed. I promised her I would go to Mexico to look for her as soon as I returned from Argentina, but that was one more promise I would not be able keep.

THE FIRE THAT IS MADE OF SHADOW IS MORE INTENSE. In the heart of darkness lives fire.

Of all the known elements on Earth fire is the most passionate one. Its body—if it's true that burnt air may be called a body—has that vertiginous undulation that only the back and the waist of a woman have. Only fire hypnotizes with its dance of untouchable red-hot flesh. Tongue of fire. Mother of destruction. Incestuous sister of death. Tongue of a woman, tongue of fire.

But not even fire can beat fire. That is why the burning of witches during the Middle Ages proved the futility of the belief which assumed that the power of a woman could be destroyed by the flames. A woman, when she is made of fire, is invincible. The witch herself is an incarnation of fire, the incarnation of a dangerous flesh, of a millenary knowledge that men fear.

In our conscience burns the bonfire of the time of truth. Fire made of somber flame is doubly intense. In the heart of doubt, in the heart of repentance, in the heart of fear lives fire. In the bonfire of the final hour burns the conscience of the flesh, the unconscious, incestuous, ephemeral flesh. In the core of the heart is the shadow that was branded there by fire.

On the days preceding my departure I decided not to call the Countess. She had never called me. She hadn't even asked for my number; she hadn't asked me for anything. She was a sex slave who had enslaved me with her insatiable lust. This is why I couldn't keep that distance.

Two days before leaving I went to look for her at the Trocadero. I got there early and ordered a beer. That night was Bondage A Go-Go Night and some of the vampiresses were already dancing on the dance floor. I found refuge in a corner to watch the girls who danced in the cages that hung from the ceiling. From this vantage point I could also see the ones who danced on the floor. I didn't want to call attention to myself. The girls had looted the shelves of Stormy Leather, the sado-masochistic boutique on Harrison Street and decorated their bodies with jewelry from Gargoyle, the store on Haight Street that announced itself as the "Purveyors of Gothic and Victorian Mysteria." They were devoted readers of Propaganda, the magazine of choice of the androgynous vampires of this dark Victorian city. Their tattoos invited speculation: could they be great-grand-daughters of Baudelaire, of Poe?

Vampires dance in a sensual and solitary way, they know themselves admired and enjoy the attention, but they do not demonstrate anything. For about an hour I entertained myself watching the scene until I discovered the Countess among the pale faces of the others. She did not see me. She went up to the second floor where there was another bar. On that floor, there was a small stage where, close to midnight, a sadomasochistic spectacle would begin. I had seen before that silly performance but it wasn't terribly interesting to me; what I lived with the Countess in private was the real thing. I tried to concentrate on the dancers in the cages and the rest who took up the center floor. I did so for another half-hour. It was easy to be entertained watching those women, who like myself hate the sun and find refuge in their solitary sensuality. But at a certain point I couldn't help going to look for the Countess. I went up the stairs and immediately realized that most of the vampires were around the torture stage. I went up to it. There were about fifty people blocking my view, but I managed to see the arms of the woman that was hanging from some chains that came down from a metal structure. Her wrists were tied with leather straps. Three vampires of barely twenty years of age surrounded her. I opened my way through the hypnotized public who watched the stage and I recognized the cat tattooed on the Countess' back on the body that hung from those chains. Her body turned slowly at the mercy of those pubescent sadists and was barely sustained by the toes of her feet on the floor of the carpeted stage. She was wearing a black leather bra that consisted barely of two or three leather straps which left her small nipples exposed and went up to her neck. Garter and silk stockings, a kind of diminutive thong that buried itself in her ass and left her white, firm cheeks exposed; on the right butt cheek the labyrinth, like a sign of doubt made of flesh. On her head, the Countess had a short black wig, with bangs, like Uma Thurman in *Pulp Fiction*, and her eyes were blindfolded with a black velvet strap.

One of the boys had a short whip with leather strips in his right hand, which he used to softly hit the back and naked ass she lifted to ease the punishment. The other used the tips of his fingers and his nails to explore her arms, armpits, and face. The third one had a kind of neon instrument with which he gave her mild electrical shocks on different parts of her body: on her bellybutton, where the Countess had a navel ring, on her neck, between her breasts and occasionally on her exposed nipples. The Countess flashed a dirty smile, licked her lips, and bit her lower one while the boy with the whip got closer to kiss her behind her right ear and asked her if everything was alright, if she wanted to continue, if he could whip her stronger. Everything happened in an absurd climate of cordiality and gentleness; she accepted to be punished, but there was a limit that she herself marked and which no one dared cross. In the back of the stage there was a young girl who was barely eighteen and was dressed in plain clothes. She was being spanked by a sinister-looking man—something which surprised me in that club where people were usually young and beautiful. But we were all looking at the Countess who was hanging in the front of the stage, at less than three feet from the spectators. Her body shone in the half-light and writhed in pleasure while the boys submitted her to their whims. After a few more lashes the boy who was behind her would put on a pair of soft black gloves, that looked like they were made of rabbit skin and caressed her tenderly where seconds earlier he had hit her. Then, taking off the gloves, he would whip her again. I took advantage of the invisibility I gained by her blindfolded eyes to drink my beer right in front of her and coldly contemplate her body and her smile. I realized that she had never been mine: she belonged to everyone. I looked at her with pride. She, the finest whore, the most feline, the most beautiful, was there, exposed by her own choice to the gaze of whoever wanted to pay fifteen dollars to get into the Trocadero. Everyone's eyes stopped freely on her nipples, on her ass, on the body that belonged to me when it was by my side. I felt an anonymous and quiet pride, but I also felt something else that I recognized as a vague disgust, a light nausea.

When I sensed that the spectacle was about to end I left the circle of voyeurs to go back down to the main floor.

I lit a cigarette and found myself bewildered. I was not angry, I didn't feel jealousy because I had no reason to feel it. On the stage on the lower floor a kind of comic opera was beginning. It was a transvestite show. I went up to the bar and ordered another beer that I didn't even touch. I wanted to get out of there before she could see me.

The night outside that twisted house of pleasure was simply one of the most beautiful I had ever seen in San Francisco.

(BAUDRILLARD TELLS THE FOLLOWING STORY: a soldier is walking near the town plaza and suddenly meets Death. When he sees her, he thinks he sees a menacing gesture in her eyes, a slight movement toward him that scares him. Running, he escapes to the palace of the King and begs him for the finest horse to flee that night to Samarkanda, far from Death's reach. The King gives him the horse and the soldier goes on his way; next thing the King sends for Death to come to the palace. When Death arrives the Monarch bitterly reproaches her for having scared one of his best soldiers, to which Death responds with an apologetic gesture: "I had no intention of scaring him, I was simply surprised to find him here since we have a date tomorrow in Samarkanda.")

No one who goes to Buenos Aires is ever disappointed.

Sabine picked me up at the airport and the meeting was as sweet as the very idea of being far from everything. She drove me in her Fiat to her Belgrano apartment and she would not stop pointing out things to me. Once there, her urgency of telling me about the most insignificant details of her return to her city and meeting again all her streets and her friends was stronger than the urgency of her body. This I was thankful for.

I was tired from the trip. From San Francisco to Miami, from Miami to São Paulo and from Brazil to her city. We talked, or rather, Sabine talked for hours while I looked out the windows of her apartment and watched people returning from work, walking their children or their dogs, taking them to the park that was in front of the building where Sabine lived. Occasionally I would interrupt her to ask her something, but Sabine was an anxious kid who overflowed as only kids can. She was also a loyal and tender sister. She felt responsible for everything: for me, for my diet, for the run-over dogs, for the Mothers of the Plaza de Mayo, for everything that was wrong in the world. At nightfall we went to bed, I kissed her eyes and fell asleep. The next day we began to stroll through the streets of her city, I started to meet her friends, and I tried to erase from myself any trace of the Countess which might still have been lingering on my fingers and on my anguish.

As soon as your eyes start to look over the streets in the downtown area you realize that Buenos Aires is not at all like the rest of Latin America. Cellular telephones in every other hand, buildings, elegant clothing and something which brings to memory other places of the world. Not the Indian Mexico of Paseo de la Reforma, unequal, with indigenous women selling arts and crafts to the German and gringo tourists in the Zona Rosa, nor the distant and opulent one of Bosques de las Lomas, where the rich live. The architecture of Buenos Aires is both spectacular and decadent, like that of Europe. The human landscape is not at all like that of indigenous America.

For some absurd reason that "being like Europe" is considered by foreigners and nationals to be something good, something to be proud of. This did not surprise me: Argentina is a nation of immigrants of European origin, more similar in its ethnic configuration to the United States or Canada, than to Bolivia or Peru. Sarmiento, during the middle of the last century, wanted this kind of immigrants. His model to follow was the United States. His formula, the same as the North Americans: eliminate the Indians and promote European immigration.

The Europeanness of Buenos Aires, that prides itself in

being the Paris of Latin America, is a product of the desire to see itself reflected in a distorted and distorting mirror. However, Menem's Buenos Aires, consumerist and subservient to foreign interests, has more to do with the frivolous vulgarity of Miami, than with the very talked about "sophistication" of Paris. The Menemist excess is not justifiable in a country where the elderly commit suicide for lack of food.

To take a stroll down Recoleta and certain areas of Palermo certainly brings to memory the urban passages more proper of Italy and Madrid than any idea one might have about South America. But the contrasts become more evident in many other parts of the city. If you cross town toward Avellaneda, if you take murderous Bus 29 towards La Boca, if you open your eyes to see beyond the fragile tinsel, then you realize the fictitious nature of that suspicious abundance.

The most traditional cafes in Buenos Aires and the old tearooms where Sabine easily dragged me were practically abandoned. They are old cafes no one goes to anymore. The fashionable places have names in English and look more like Los Angeles than a place on the most Austral point of the continent.

What terrible insecurity lies in the depths of this shiny and plastic surface?

We slowly wandered through the city. Slowly we got to know each other again. I was relieved of having escaped from my anguish. She was excited about showing me a city she was in love with.

I didn't know where to start getting acquainted with her town. I wanted to go to the place where Sabato sat to watch the park trails that would bring his characters to look for him. I wanted to run into the ghosts of Borges and Bioy Casares on the street and witness their phantasmagoric dialogue. I wanted an Argentina I could not find in the three weeks of my stay, an electric tango that would hit me in the veins, a line of a poem.

Sabine showed me off to her friends. There I was exotic. I was older than they were, and I spoke a different Spanish. Also, I lived in the United States and they all wanted to know about California. I never enjoyed talking about California when I was abroad. On the one hand, I was bothered by that adoration many young people, especially in far away countries such as Brazil or now Argentina, seemed to have for the country that, in a way, was greatly responsible for them not having decent jobs. On the other hand, in many places in Latin America, starting in Mexico, people who ask about life in the United States seem to be under the impression that all Mexicans who live in the Northern country were some sort of slaves who had to step off the sidewalks (like the Indians of Chiapas in San Cristóbal de las Casas) so that the white people could walk by. In a world so full of stereotypes and clichés this was understandable, but by no means less uncomfortable.

However, I was tolerant and complacent. Sabine took me everywhere and I kept my eyes open looking for cafes and bookstores where I could spend my time and my money in the best possible way. I could not believe the beauty of the women of Buenos Aires who that summer sported their anorexic thighs with killer miniskirts. This amused Sabine.

The second morning I went down to buy newspapers at the kiosk on the corner. *La Nación, Clarín, página/12*. It was a Sunday. In the literary section of *La Nación* the ubiquitous Carlos Fuentes, who appeared just as easily in the *New York Times* as in *Le Monde*, was talking about Chiapas and the Zapatistas; in *página/12* Galeano and Benedetti repeated themselves ad infinitum; in *Clarín*, Menem's ex, Zulema, demanded, with a gesture of aggravation and too much makeup in the picture, that new investigations be conducted on the accidental death of her son Carlitos, who had killed himself in a private helicopter that the Argentinean people had subsidized so that the boy could play on the weekends with his friends. What's new pussycat?

But I was not ready for this: in a small lost square, on a random page of *página/12*, a paid ad reproduced the photograph of one of the "disappeared." Not someone who had disappeared two weeks ago, but someone from the era of the dictatorship. The text read something along the lines of "We do not forget you, we demand justice" and some other things I do not recall, not because I had not read it over and over again, but rather because the shock of that absurd reality hit me in an unexpected way. I looked for other similar ads and found them. Young faces, some of them smiling, most of them beautiful.

"Have you seen this?" I asked Sabine, who was preparing her *mate* in the kitchen.

"Yeah. They always show up," she answered, but not as if I should have known something of such a daily nature in her city, but as if avoiding an explanation.

I returned to the table where I was reading. I read each one of the ads. I was touched and imagined one of the Mothers of the Plaza de Mayo going to the newspaper office to pay for the ad with the few pesos of her retirement paycheck, month after month, year after year.

I lit a cigarette and saw through the window a mother playing with her children. And I, would I have children some day? I thought that, just like that young mother, the mothers of the disappeared had, some day in the past, taken their children to play in the park; possibly that same park.

"What are you thinking about?" Sabine came out of the kitchen, sipping her *mate* through the silver straw.

"About the children that I will never have, merely on account of my cowardice."

Days later, I don't know why, we left the streets and parks of the city and went to Patagonia.

AND WHAT IS A PHOTOGRAPH IF NOT A TATTOO?

Frozen smiles that hurt. Photographs of childhood; your mother young again; your father with his hand on your shoulder. A music of vanished signs, of hair that turned white or never even had the time to do so. The photographs of the dead are tattoos that the eyes and time leave upon happiness and repentance.

What did I not say?

I am in a hospital bed, that is, in the waiting room to hell. The same logos that granted me the ephemeral pleasure of another's flesh has hit me with the reality of a useless body. My logos, my *raison de étre*, was desire. Now my only desire is that my memories can be like those tattoos made out of light which I kissed with respectful, dry lips: fertile signs.

The hospital smells like death. It smells like wounded flesh. Like time and ruin. But there is no wound of the flesh that is as great and as filthy as this rotting of the soul.

PATAGONIA IS AN OCEAN OF BUSHES and dry grazing lands.

It is an extension of interminable land that must be crossed to get to the end of the world.

We drove for fifteen hours at a scary average speed of 100 miles per hour in Sabine's car that was gliding as if on velvet roads.

At a certain point in the road a sign announced PATAGONIA BEGINS HERE and immediately after it, the next sign read THE MALVINAS BELONG TO ARGENTINA (however, in a movie I saw with Sabine when we returned to Buenos Aires, the same sign read THE MALVINAS BELONG TO THE PENGUINS— someone with a good sense of humor had altered the nationalist legend). I would have liked to stop but I reacted too late to take a picture. This fact didn't bother me too much since the most important images are those imprinted upon the mind of the traveler, the mental pictures.

We drove for hours and found absolutely nothing on the road, except cargo trucks headed for or returning from the South. We saluted them with the enthusiasm of an accomplice. Next to the road there were no signs of life. I did not perceive the presence of birds, although later in Comodoro Rivadavia, our most Austral destination and where some relatives of Sabine's lived, I bought a recording of over sixty native birds of Patagonia, which destroyed my theory that birds did not venture into this remote area of the continent.

There is a whole mythology built around Patagonia unknown outside of certain interested circles. In the personal library of one of Sabine's uncles I found a book which tells the story of the first colonizers of European origin who arrived to these lands and described the presence of giants who were almost ten feet tall. Of course the distance between reality and fantasy is enormous in stories like this one. The truth is that the remoteness of this region invites speculation. To drive through Patagonia is a magical experience. Patagonia is an ocean of ashes.

We arrived at Comodoro Rivadavia, so called in honor of the sailor who found oil when he was looking for water on these arid planes, and we installed ourselves in the house of one of Sabine's aunts who gave us one room, though seeming quite uncomfortable with the idea of letting us sleep together without being married. Comodoro is the most important city of this region of Argentina and it is famous for its strategic location during the war over the "Falkland" Islands (according to the British) or the "Malvinas" (according to the Argentineans) at the beginning of the last decade. Many remember the night when the usurping, murderous president, Galtieri, appeared drunk on television to announce, in a thick voice, that his country—then governed by a military junta—had declared war on one of the largest military and economic powers of the world, Great Britain. The drunken general sent hundreds of young Argentineans to a stupid and unnecessary death. On the islands, those who did not die of cold and hunger were massacred by an English army that finally felt sorry for them and ended up giving them the food and clothing their own government denied them, because the Argentinean military had been inept and corrupt even at waging war.

The memory of this war still lives on in Comodoro, where the people, though they try not to speak of those times very often, have suffered the construction, initiative of the local authorities, of horrible monuments in honor of the glorious Argentinean army which adorn the coastal avenue of the city. Nothing more idiotic than a monument to the Unknown Soldier: at eighteen, that soldier had a mother and a girlfriend. That soldier was somebody, he was known.

It was precisely when we were walking along the sea looking at the statues that I asked Sabine about those years of the "Dirty War." I had already tried to do so in Buenos Aires, but something interrupted our conversation. According to my calculations, Sabine was only a child when the dictatorship tore apart the country and killed thousands of young people. I asked her what her family had done during those years, but Sabine answered with silence, and I felt disconcerted.

"Why don't you answer?"

She looked into my eyes and suddenly she blushed.

"*Mierda*. Why the hell does everyone have to ask me about those fucking years?" she answered with a violence I had never before seen in her.

She started walking and I followed her without knowing what to do or what to say; her anger was unjustified in my eyes. The icy wind blew and made our hair fly about. We were almost at the end of the world and the strong wind reminded us of this almost twenty-four hours a day.

"You don't have to get like that. I was only asking you a question."

"And what do you want me to say? There are some things I don't talk about, period." She almost yelled at me in a voice drowned out by a wave that was crashing on a nearby beach.

I suddenly sensed that there was something rotten behind her reaction and that intuition filled me with doubts and bitter suspicion. I postponed my questions for a more propitious moment.

We didn't stay in Comodoro for very long. Three days later we drove back three hours due north towards the ranch her family owned in a region called Camarones. I felt like we were entering a territory that had no place in this century. That ranch was a small country unto itself. Over twenty-five thousand Australian sheep lived over an extension of one hundred thousand acres of dry, gloomy land. There were wild horses, ostriches, maras, guanacos, and chulengos. An English-style mansion presided over the property from atop a hill. The gauchos were finishing the shearing of the last sheep and the ranch administrator, an old German who attentively made sure that we lacked nothing, would slaughter a lamb for us daily, to have it roasted on a pit fire. The only thing missing was the legendary gaucho Martín Fierro.

On the ranch Sabine returned to her normal self. I imagined, only for an instant, a life by her side, away from everything. I would become an anachronic feudal master, dedicated to reading. But I hated the silence of that remote place, that extension of land I would never explore, and immediately discarded the idea. I needed the city with its secret daily rhythms, the artifice and simulacrum of its window displays, the illusion of that world of steel and showcases. I would never understand country life. My contemporary abnormality, my unnatural being, lived in perfect harmony in its habitat of sounds coming from streets and gas stations, and cappuccinos around the corner. A life like that, in the country, would end up ruining my life and I would end up becoming a poet out of pure boredom.

Sabine spent the next three days sunbathing on the terrace and I spent the time writing letters and looking through the books of the house library.

CONSTANCIA,

you will never read this letter I write to you from a forbidden place. it does not matter; in a way, writing to you has always been my way of getting close, not to you, but to my idea of what I feel for you.

today I woke up feeling your presence. your eyes of water woke me with their absent demand. then, the woman you do not know I'm with in the farthest and strangest of places, ran her fingers through my hair and said good morning. as her fingers touched me I felt the weight of treason as I had never felt it before.

I fled from myself only to discover that I cannot flee from myself. as in that Cavafis poem, the city has followed me, has pursued me, has surrounded me in a corner of the world, the farthest of them all.

now they have brought me tea and that has brought the memory of another woman made of air. I do not know where she is because her eyes go where air goes. you know about her, but you do not know that she is waiting for me.

I have an exact memory of every inch of your skin, each word spoken and written by my hand, a hand totally in love with you.

149

your body, like our city, is a landscape that I now miss. here I see the opposite landscape, you know? everything here is backwards, even the sky. our mexican cafes, our parks, our hotel beds, everything is far. guilt takes me far away from you.

you don't know that I fell into a pit, I never told you about it. you don't know that I entered a labyrinth and that my entire body is burned. I would need your body of water to appease this pain that borders on the truly intolerable. do you know what the most odious thing is? that this fire was a mirror. I saw in that mirror made of flesh and smoke a face I should have never seen.

I saw myself in the black waters of that pit and I cannot deny how much I enjoyed that image of rotting skin, that desire to fall into the depths, to get lost in the velvet-covered hallways of a carnal labyrinth where the minotaur awaits at the end. I saw the minotaur straight ahead of me and in his eyes I recognized my own.

but I do not feel fear. I feel guilt.

do you remember the nightmare? no, I think I wanted to tell you about it at some point and for some reason that escapes me now I did not. it is one of those recurrent nightmares; it returns at times of my life dominated by intensity. it is probably a nightmare I deserve. In it I am standing on a field and have my eyes fixed on something in the distance which begins to take shape. first it is a distant dot that grows little by little. it is a dark dot of gradually increasing size. behind the dot there is some sort of smoke. I see that and begin to feel an uneasiness that increases as the dot ceases to be a dot to become a mass whose shape I begin to distinguish. seconds that seem like years go by and the mass joins a rhythmic sound that starts to become a vibration. the mass acquires precise shape and color: it is a black bull. I cannot move. I am hypnotized by its eyes and by the rhythm of its crazed dash towards me. it is headed directly towards me and my mouth gets dry. the uneasiness is now panic. I want to run and my legs do not respond. the smoke is in reality a dust storm born at its galloping hooves and the sound grows, the volume increases and the bull arrives, arrives to where I am waiting an eternal wait. from its chops the beast drips a violent drool and its eyes look at me with a hatred my fear does not understand. it arrives and charges me, it buries its horns deep in my chest and in that moment Constancia, always, always in that moment, I wake up screaming.

that is my nightmare, and I should have told it to you so that you could understand me.

and now I cannot even send you this letter, because everything in my life has become forbidden.

We returned to Buenos Aires.

I had our fight by the sea stuck in my chest. Walking once again with her around Belgrano I couldn't help asking her the question once again. I had seen many things I could not understand. I knew, through Sabine's casual comments, that her father was the owner of some companies in the South. I had seen with my own eyes the gigantic ranch. Her family owned land in four or five different places in the country and little by little I was finding out details that led me to deduce that there was more, perhaps much more I did not know about.

At a street corner I took her by the shoulders and whispered the question again.

"I want you to tell me what your family did during the time the military was in power."

Sabine looked at me coldly.

"If you truly love me, you will have to stop asking," she answered.

We continued walking.

That afternoon, when we went back to her apartment,

Sabine immediately locked herself in one of the rooms and I began drinking wine while listening to her sobs through the door. I tried several times to get her to open the door but she paid no attention to me. I continued drinking. An hour later Sabine came out of the room with puffy eyes and her hair falling about her face.

"Come with me," she said, indicating the entrance to the kitchen. I followed her.

She put on a kettle of water for her *mate*.

"There are some things which not even I have dared ask about," she said in a voice broken by an hour of weeping. "Do you know what they tell you here when you question the fucking military? When you ask about the tortures and the killings? 'One does not speak of that, dear...' What the hell do you think? That I don't ask myself about these things, that I don't want to know, that I don't care? Do you think that I don't wish to know what the fuck my old man did during those years? Or what my uncles, my aunts, my neighbors, my best friend's parents did? You have no idea what the hell it feels like to ask about that..."

She stopped as if she realized that she was saying too much.

I tried to approach her, but she rejected me.

"Look," she said, and showed me two fine scars on her wrists, which I had never noticed. "Why do you think I was given a trip to California? Because I was not able to kill myself, that's why, you son of a bitch. Because after all it is easier to buy silence than give clear answers to two or three questions."

She prepared her *mate* and added a little milk.

The kitchen window faced the park. There, some mothers played with their children and Sabine watched them attentively while she sipped her *mate*.

"My father was never in the military," she continued, "but in a country like this one...." She paused again.

"And what do you want to know?" I risked the question.

"Who am I. That's all. Where do I come from." Finally, she collapsed in my arms and wept clean tears.

The mothers and their children continued to play in the park.

From their silence, my own unborn children asked me the question that had never before had an answer.

"God, life is such a bitch." I took out a handkerchief and cleaned her nose.

IF ONE TRAVELS GUIDED ONLY BY INTUITION, one enters with one eye closed and one eye open into the territory of chance and open interpretation of the fact. In that territory all is fair, any theory counts.

The experiences lived during that trip were ambiguous. To wake up one morning, read the paper, and discover that in the 90s the mothers of those disappeared during the dictatorship continue to publish pictures of their children in the papers. To walk through the city of Buenos Aires in the dark and discover that I was living, with Sabine by my side, a scene from a Pino Solanas' movie called *Sur* and receive that discovery in a shudder and as if touched by lightning. To visit La Boca and see scenes possible only in the novels of the Uruguayan Juan Carlos Onetti, in his *Astillero*. To coincide one night on Avenida Corrientes with hundreds of River Plate fans who run enthusiastically toward the Obelisco at the intersection of Nueve de Julio and Corrientes to celebrate the triumph of their team in the soccer championship. Or to simply chat at a cafe with friends until five o'clock in the morning. Simple things. For a few days I was almost able to forget the labyrinth.

THREE WEEKS IN ARGENTINA WERE ENOUGH for something permanent to begin to take root between Sabine and I. She told me that she would return to San Francisco to be closer to me and in this I heard something else. I heard that she wanted to be far from her doubts about her family and about her origin. On the other hand, Sabine was convinced that she could domesticate me and thanks to this I began toying with the idea that some day I would have to stop chasing tattoos.

However, three weeks were not enough to make me forget Constancia's eyes, which I needed more than ever, nor my sister of air who never demanded from me anything other than my honesty. I tried to forget the Countess. But the images of what we did in our savage encounters assaulted me. A couple of times I had to make a great effort in order to control my desire to bite Sabine and dig my fingernails into her. It would have been a transgression, an unforgivable attack; more unforgivable after what had happened the night she confessed her suicide attempt.

I LEFT BUENOS AIRES WITH A PLAN SKETCHED IN MY HEAD. I was not very convinced that I would carry it out to the letter, but at least I would try it out, I told myself.

I would talk with Marianne and explain my relationship with Sabine. I could not tell her a thing about Constancia or the Countess, but it would not be necessary; she would understand because she understood everything. As I thought about this I understood that Marianne was someone who wanted me to be free to make my own choices. I also thought that maybe in the end I was afraid to surrender to her because that would force me to be free and I would not know what to do with that. That is why I hadn't gone with her to travel the world. Few things can be as terrible as freedom.

I would not see the Countess again. My addiction to her was such that I was certain I would sink once more into that incredibly dangerous, dark pit.

I did not know what explanation I would give Constancia. She knew about Marianne and Sabine. It had all been so unexpected between us that our future was too uncertain. She in Mexico and I in California. Too much distance between the two points, between the two bodies. I would have to convince myself that the past was unrecoverable in order to kill the illusion of going back to Mexico City. To renounce her equaled renouncing my memory; but all the self-sacrifices are always, in some way, justifiable.

Buenos Aires was a tempting possibility in my future. Sabine proposed that after getting a Masters in the United States (and that was the pretext she would use to justify her return to San Francisco, which her parents would not completely believe since they had briefly met me) the two of us would go live in Buenos Aires together. I did not dislike the idea. I could look for a position at some university in Buenos Aires, write my books, and live the life I had barely tasted during those three weeks. Perhaps some day we would even have kids who would speak a strange blend of Argentinean and Mexican Spanish. Kids. Damn. Three or four, according to her. One would be too much, according to me.

I took the plane back, firmly resolved to start changes so that when Sabine returned to San Francisco my life would be different.

But I wrote those plans on a surface made out of air, of water, of fire.

ACCORDING TO THIS SOUTH AMERICAN WRITER, Miami is the cultural capital of Latin America. When I heard him say that during a writer's conference, my Latin Americanist pride rebelled violently against such a dreadful declaration. But now in Miami (where I had to spend the night because the flight was delayed four hours in Brazil and I lost my connection to San Francisco), strolling once again through the old downtown area and the beach, I understood the reason for the writer's observation. I had seen symptoms of that Miamization of Latin America in Mexico, and was just returning from enduring them in Buenos Aires. Everywhere there were immigrants and tourists from Latin America and the Caribbean. Spanish was spoken in every accent and variant imaginable. Something in the air, undeniable to me, gave this town a unique character, impossible to find elsewhere in America. I had been in Miami in transit to Brazil some years ago and once again I did not like it. Just as a few years ago, in my rented car, I drove those streets, that coastal avenue, that pastel-colored artifice made up of Art Deco buildings, jolly seniors, clothing by the late

Versace (the favorite bitch designer of Menem's millionaire bitches), and tanned headless bodies. Perhaps that writer was right and in a way this was the capital of Latin America. But believing that means that the future of Latin America will be (although it already is in some places) a poor and distorted version of this frivolous Babel, empire of bad taste, deceitful entry to modern Rome.

After Miami, returning to San Francisco is pure bliss.

EVERY MORNING, SAN FRANCISCO WEARS A VEIL OF FOG. From the ocean comes a dense, cool fog that slowly crosses through the Golden Gate to advance like a lover's hand over the body of the Bay until it reaches the piers, the hills, the Victorian houses, the financial district towers. It is a thick caress that takes the sun hours to destroy. The fog creates the sensation of living in a contradictory cloud, since the image of San Francisco is that of a city more properly belonging to creatures of the night than to angels walking on clouds. How can angels and vampires share the same streets? San Francisco, destroyed at the beginning of the 20th century by earthquake and fire, and reborn from its ashes, is a blind and generous mother who loves all her creatures.

There is no city more feminine than this one, sitting at the window of fog on the "left side of the world," as Lawrence Ferlinghetti, the greatest poet of this almost fractured island, calls this barbaric coast. Some day the earth will swallow it. Some day all of us, angels and night creatures, will be devoured with her by the geological faults that desire her.

That is the reason for this climate of suspense. This sweet waiting.

IF YOU WANT GOD TO LAUGH, you go tell him about your plans.

When I called Marianne I was surprised not to find her home at midnight. I left a message on her answering machine and went to bed. The next day she called. Would you like to go out for a drink? At seven, at Bruno's.

We gave each other a long hug. We were truly happy to see each other again. She told me how she was doing with her photographs. She was working on a photo documental about the Chinatown of San Francisco and said she wanted to show me some of the pictures. As for myself, I did not avoid the topic of Buenos Aires, but I was very careful with what I said. I noticed that she seemed worried.

"There is something you are not telling me dear," I told her.

"I think there are things both of us are not saying." She looked into my eyes and took my hand.

I took a deep breath and lit a cigarette.

"Why not say it now?" I asked her with a knot growing in my throat.

"I met a wonderful man," she said.

I was not ready for that. Only a few seconds before I had speculated that something in my demeanor had betrayed me and that I would have to spend the next half-hour justifying Sabine's existence in my life. The waitress came over and I asked for another round of martinis. Marianne's eyes were bluer than ever.

"Do you want to tell me about it?" I asked again, taking a deep breath.

"There is not much to tell. I have been seeing him quite frequently during the past few days and I began to realize that he is very much in love with me. You know, he gives me his time and his attention and that is very flattering. During these last two months since my arrival, I have barely seen you. When I am here you are traveling and vice versa. And now that I have not been traveling during the last few weeks this happens to me. I am confused because I still love you, though this feeling I have for you is not really reciprocated other than with the notion that you love me too. I am afraid that is not enough."

"Are you sleeping with him?" I was about to lose my voice.

"That is not the point. But if you must know, the answer is no. We have kissed but it has gone no further. He knows about you, he respects my decision to wait until you and I have defined what we want to do about us, and has been equally respectful towards me. You know, he doesn't pressure me and that is something most women appreciate wholeheartedly."

"I am sorry, but I had to ask you that damn question before it burned me up inside. Not now, but some time in the future, I also have things I want to get off my chest. Right now, I can't."

"Another woman?" Now she was the one lighting a cigarette.

"Yes, but if you give me the chance to explain it another time, I would really appreciate it."

"OK. Whenever you feel ready."

"And if you don't mind, that is enough for now. I am not angry, nor could I be, Marianne. But it is not a good time."

"I don't think there is such a thing as a 'good time' to talk about these things, but I am not going to force you to talk about anything." Her voice turned dry.

I realized that my confirmation about the existence of another woman had bothered her. I asked for the check and we left without touching the drinks the waitress had just brought.

On the way to her house, where she asked me to take her, I began to cry almost without realizing it. I stopped the car and Marianne lovingly hugged me. "Forgive me," she said. "No," I answered, sobbing, "forgive me." And I started to cry as I had not cried in over twenty years. And the tears were not enough to cleanse me from all the fucking adult filth, all the guilt, all the bitterness.

"My god... what a bloody mess..." Marianne said out loud to herself.

THIS IS MY FRAIL EMPIRE: my luminous memory of four women, three cats, and a useless body.

Four erotic cities which together form the capital city of my confused universe. A universe of physical ruin, lost harem and hospital.

One is the cosmic, aerial, borderless city. City where I could have been free and was not brave enough to do so, so I could go everywhere with her. City of fraternal love where Narcissus would not see his sister dead but would learn to see her true face and no longer the trickery of his own image. City without simulacrum, without distorting mirror, without labyrinth and without pit. Photograph of time captured by smiles and steps without set destination. Of streets that meet all the doors, plazas, and parks. Of forests which are not for hunting, or seeking prey. Cosmopolis of the open senses. City open to all the members of the tribe, Marianne, for me as well, who was afraid to be free and now evoke that minute of indecision with something that is not even sadness. Cosmic city of the East, engraved with a panther. City of air.

City of water founded on water. City origin of life and endangered center of the universe. Navel, waist, genital metropolis. Mother city made of liquid substance where one reclaims an alphabet of comprehensible, decipherable signs. All your cities lead to the ocean, aquatic city. All your plazas, the plaza of your belly, the plaza of your legs, and the sacred main plaza of your sex, lead through secret rivers to the original lake, the culture medium for Genesis. Glass of transparent truths. Water made of familiar language, of moan that is waterfall, of kiss that is crashing of waves, of caress that is stream of crystalline laughter. Eyes made of gray water, primary woman, of water, transparent presence whose memory refreshes and caresses. Constancia: woman city made of water, tattooed with the water of my mouth and my lost words.

Black fire, Western city of the Apocalypse. In your intricate alleys, in your humid labyrinths, in the pit of your sex, in the pit of your gross and insatiable anus there is a net of pleasant roads that lead to the center of hell. *Fin de siècle* bitch. Decadent daughter of rotten Western decay, of Western rust and urine. You have no name, or your name is the flame of singed flesh, whip of excessive appetite, deranged feline, tiger of the forest of death, oven that broils serenity, burner of the fingers, bonfire of the instincts. Northern, gothic, vampire city. Not even the water which surrounds your waist has any power over the dark bonfire where the velvet of your cunt is burning, the silk of your bad intentions, the premeditated fingernail of your detachment, the enigmatic mark of your labyrinth, the howling of your cat in eternal heat. The fire dances its sensual dance of masks and simulacrum, its ritual of artifice. And in the center of your trickery lives the shame of needing you and not feeling repentance and wanting more. Such is the nature of that fire. Reticent citizen of the city of fire, the earth opened under my feet and I fell into the pit of the fiery belly of the beast.

South. Southern City. I return South as one always returns to love. Land of uncertain future. Closes the circle of restlessness and in closing it destroys it with its hand over its forehead. In your untouched belly awaits the seed of possibilities. In the ruin and the happiness over your firm land alights the hope of a Phoenix bird attempting to escape the labyrinth. From your ankle buds a delicate branch and my gaze circles it and my hand touches it like one of my fingers touches your mouth. Root of the answers, you extend into my night your subterranean stalks, you sink, into the dark ground of my fear, the root of light that blinds the worms that inhabit me and restores the solidity to my spine, to my present of deserved decadence. Deep and necessary, generous as a furrow, sonorous and fertile like your voice, which has an echo of distance, but calls me, and reaches me, and wishes to rescue me.

I TRIED TO RETURN TO MY NORMAL LIFE but as the weekend grew near I began experiencing four distinct kinds of
anxiety.

The first had to do with the sudden absence of
Marianne, the unexpected dividing line that had been
imposed by the events, product of my negligence. I could
not blame her; she loved me but I was dealing in an
obscurity unknown to her.

The second anxiety was the result of my nostalgia for
Sabine. I had lived in Buenos Aires in such an intense way
that I couldn't understand why I hadn't sent everything to
hell to find eternal refuge from myself in a new country, a
new life. Cavafis was smiling.

The third was rooted in Mexico. Constancia and I had
fantasized about my return to Mexico and that return was
uncertain since Sabine would soon come to San
Francisco. Also, when Constancia had attempted to come,
I had unintentionally boycotted that attempt with my
inopportune decision to take off to Argentina fleeing the
fire labyrinth of the Countess. And she, the Countess, was

the cause of the fourth anxiety.

The weekend was nearing and I knew that on Saturday's full moon she would be at the Trocadero, her nipples wearing the makeup of my desire. She was a witch, a woman of fire, and I felt the calling of her flesh nailing itself in my stomach, like an order.

And as if four were not enough, a fifth anxiety added itself to the first four. The previous night, before bedtime, while I was writing a letter to Constancia telling her about my ambivalent feelings regarding the future of our relationship, and perhaps hoping that she would leave me, a sharp pain in my head made me fall to the ground. For a few seconds I feared the worst. Nothing similar had ever happened to me. The pain was indescribable, it came from the deepest recesses of my skull and I found myself on the floor grabbing my head with both hands, my forehead covered in cold sweat and suffering shivers throughout my entire body.

When the pain began to subside, an absurd scene suddenly entered my imagination. The Countess, naked in her house, was pinning a needle in the head of a wax doll.

It took me a few minutes to feel better. My cats slowly came over to me, halfway between scared and worried. I had on my closed eyes the image of Marianne's tattoo, the piercing eyes of the panther on her back; the labyrinth on the Countess' ass, her whimsical cat looking at me with defiance, smiling; the golden branch on Sabine's ankle; the tattoo of my ephemeral words devoured by Constancia's body. An impossible needle in a wax doll. I was scared. I saw Narcissus, dead by the side of the pond struck in the head by an arrow. Legión was licking my hand and meowed in dismay. Cordelia looked at me from a timid distance. Fuensanta was sitting on my chest and licked her fur like an Egyptian goddess, cruel and indifferent.

LABYRINTH—INTO WHAT?

In the center of the labyrinth a man digs a pit, falls into it and is not able to get out. And if he were able to, then what?

In the center of the labyrinth, in the very center of the bullfight ring, a tattooed man examines the inscriptions on his body. On his chest a scar in the shape of a question mark. A stupid accident, he remembers. No. There was never an accident. He would not be able to remember an accident. For years he has been trying to convince himself that his scar was the product of an accident in order to force himself to forget that afternoon in the bullring of La Florecita. Who was he then? An amateur, a novice, a stupid kid and nothing more. There is no greater glory than that of a bullfighter, he had always told himself. But that afternoon he had drunk too much and his friends were not able to stop him before he jumped into the ring during a bullfight. Looking for a glory he did not deserve, he took a cape that was lying on one of the barriers and hurried towards the bull. The public booed his farce and the collective rejection inflamed him. The stare of the bull standing directly in front of him penetrated him and melted his bones. He called out to it with a drunken shout and when the bull's deep eyes took hold of his and identified him as an impostor he knew of nothing else. He woke up in a hospital and threw up. He made himself sick. But he was lucky. There is no greater glory than that of a bullfighter, but there was never greater ridicule than his. He was lucky because the bull's horn did not perforate any vital organs. Two broken ribs and a horrible rip on the skin of his chest that left him that curious scar in the shape of a question mark. Pasiphaë's bull was more productive. That was the reason for the labyrinth. That was the reason for the pursuit of signs. That was the reason for the artifice and the trickery. He was his own Minotaur and at the same time he had engendered his confinement in that enigma without an answer. There is no greater anguish than that of the monstrous bastard who travels his empire howling his desire and his appetite. Bull, father of doubt and of death. He couldn't be Narcissus because Narcissus was beautiful. He was the product of that undesired scar and that is why he sought voluntary scars, chosen scars. A panther whose scent was bewitching; a voluptuous and hypocritical cat; a branch on golden skin; a body tattooed with saliva and ink. Tattoos of air and water. Tattoos of earth and fire. The labyrinth, house of the hunt. The pit, dark, immobile, certain presence. In that Mexican hospital he decided that it was better to go abroad than tolerate the ridicule. To take his scar and his shame abroad. Any excuse would be enough.

I HAD A PREMONITION OF RUIN, a sign I could not ignore. How many times had I chosen not to listen to the signs? Now one of them was here with a message of intense pain, drilling into my brain.

In case of accident or emergency please call... Whom? I am alone in a foreign land. Call Constancia and tell her not to come. Call Sabine and tell her not to come. Call my parents, my friend Gustavo, my neighbor, the Irish widow who feeds my cats when I am away?

I didn't want to go to see a doctor. There is no prescription against the labyrinth. There is no diet to control this kind of appetite.

The pain did not return for two weeks. I sat at my desk where my essay on García Ponce had barely benefited from that pause during which I did not drink, I did not seek anyone, and I did not leave for anything other than minor, everyday chores.

One afternoon I went for a walk in Golden Gate Park. It was still winter and the afternoon fog was already coming around to fondle the treetops. I saw a father with his son playing catch with a ball and a baseball mitt. I could have a son that age, I told myself. At thirty-five I could have a teenage son. The idea depressed me. A dog came over to me, jumping around and wagging its tail; I ordered it away. Its owner looked at me with anger without understanding how someone could not want to start a conversation with her fucking dog. A beggar asked me for money and while I gave him a coin I asked myself if that man had sometime lived in a labyrinth like mine. A couple of lovers walked by in the opposite direction; she looked at me and I guessed a shiver in her eyes. If I could have seen myself I would have understood the reason for that reaction. Dark gray trenchcoat. Dark glasses. Long loose hair, and a wool scarf to protect myself against the icy San Francisco wind. Black shirt and slacks. My face, contorted by nights of poor sleep, seemed to be marked by the internal signs that tortured me.

I sat on a bench to smoke and in that instant I wished as never before a life in Mexico like that of my brother: kids, soccer games on weekends, Sunday meals with my parents. Or a life in Buenos Aires with Sabine, with friends and long nights of conversations in old cafes. Or that eternal voyage by Marianne's side with light luggage, without the compromise of spiritual mortgages. Or a house in Oaxaca with Constancia and lazy afternoons to read, and maybe write books. I desired each one of the things I could no longer have. The tattoos are not marks upon the skin, they are marks upon the idea that one has about oneself, I told myself. I had tattooed my chest with another scar. Everything is a question.

I wanted to find answers in the signs, but the very nature of the signs and their final meaning can become indecipherable if seen through the eyes of desperation. Someone would have to come and help me decipher them.

Who would come? Or had that person arrived and I was not able to realize it?

I knew at that moment that I could not evade the sign that had marked my entire life. I knew that I was the owner of a small empire made out of fog and flesh, like this city lying on the shore of the Pacific. I was a foreigner without a language and with a blurry map; without his own air, his own land, his own water, without water in a *fin de siècle* desert, tortured by the fire of doubt, the fire of open-ended questions, the fire of the writing of signs upon the skin.

I remember it all well from my hospital bed because it happened only a few days ago. I put out the cigarette and went to hunt for the Countess in her hideous labyrinth.

TWO BODIES TOUCHING EACH OTHER. What do fingers know? Whisper of kiss on the breath, nose touches crease of mouth, lip, chin. One of us closes eyes, the other watches, would like to decipher, guess the images of the private film projected upon those nervous lids. One remembers the sea, that same sea which is the origin. The other remembers nothing, surrenders to that exchange of saliva, to that tasting of tongue and teeth, to that consciousness of hands going up the back, ascending, descending, discovering incredibly soft textures. One is incredulity and thankfulness. The other is pure pleasure, feline and selfish.

Two bodies touching. Erect nipples, moist in the vaginal lips as dew blooming in the morning cold upon the petals of red roses. Erection of the flesh that seeks its better refuge.

What does the flesh know?

Did you miss me? No, I did not miss you, but I needed your body, or any body, a couple of times.

What is fear, if not the open recognition of failure? There is no such thing as absolute possession. To discover this is to acknowledge the futility of the passion that wants exclusivity, ownership. Not even your body, scar of all your desires, belongs to you. In your eyes I see how your pupils dilate. Then I see your trembling lips. My hands explore the insides of your thighs, the incredibly fine skin of the insides of your thighs. I think that I would like to make love to you softly, penetrate you slowly and make love to you with delicate movements while you love me. But I could not disappoint you. The pact is different and we both know it. Love cannot exist between us. I have to use you and you have to pay me back with pleasure, your pleasure. You could expect nothing else from me other than that business of the bodies, that honest transaction of fluids and moans that arise from both of us when I place my cock in its entirety inside of you in a sudden attack which seeks to surprise you. Then your fingernails dig into my back and your child bitch voice says: "Fuck me hard baby, fuck me hard." And I obey while suddenly the memory of Constancia's body comes over me and I drown the feeling of betrayal looking for your nipples with my lips. I flee love because to flee is the privilege of cowards and I decide to flee from that other body by hiding my lips in your skin.

I am afraid of failing you because my vanity is greater than my desire to not fuck you like this. I would prefer to kiss with slow tenderness every inch of this body I have punished in many ways during so many drunk nights over this winter. But you would scorn my weakness. That is why I bite your breasts so hard while your fingernails dig into my neck. I lift your legs and put your calves on my shoulders. Grabbing onto the mattress, covered in burgundy-colored satin sheets, I start a movement that seeks to split you in half. I fuck you with a force you oppose by pushing your hips towards me every time I advance. I feel the bone of your pelvis on mine and feel my coldness. I think of sex as an unavoidable tragedy. I go into a state of mind, the kind that is only caused by the saddest of tangos and begin to bite your right calf.

I miss Sabine, Constancia, and Marianne, but you do not know this, nor do you care. You moan while I watch myself from some region in a broken distance. What will kill me? Guilt or desire? Fuck me from behind, fuck me doggie style, you ask me, you order me as I feel that aroma of smoke rising from your hair. You turn and kneel in front of me while your hips become as wide as my awareness of your forbidden name.

I called you Countess because somehow you are a descendant of the Marquis and all in you is a decadent, corrupt, pleasurable game. The form is the content and the form of your ass confirms the content of this pit. From the marked surface of your ass the labyrinth looks at me with its eye, its vertigo, and its enigma. Your anus shines clean and soft like the perfect center of a black rose whose perfume inebriates, bewilders, stupefies.

This is an untranslatable sign. Desire is an untranslatable sign. I enter you and close my eyes. Your flesh tightens around my erect cock, its ephemeral nourishment. You would suck my blood if I were to offer it to you, and what else, other than my blood, have I offered you, my vampiress? I take you by your shoulders and push my body into yours. I remember a dream with a bull and a bellowing and I am suddenly afraid. I remember a perfect smile at barely two feet from a mirror, an ink made of Portuguese wine, a body made of water. I remember the image of my face, lightly wet by the New York rain, a flash, another smile. A park in Buenos Aires where my unborn children do not play with their mother. But this semen which swells my testicles, your fingernails that leave the nape of your neck to forcefully dig into the back of my hands, remind me of the brutal deeds of my appetite and force me to open my eyes.

I stand before a mirror and my name is Narcissus. I am a tattoo hunter. My name is whatever you want it to be. Dark sister, you did not have any traps made of velvet, your flesh was not a net. I am my own trap, I begin to tell myself while a sharp and familiar pain, which comes from inside my brain, takes over my body. Everything becomes blurry and I close my eyes again. I see a labyrinth and the smile of a cat. The cat looks at me from its indifference. San Francisco and this woman's flesh begin to vanish as, after the pain, darkness arrives with its silence.